An Advent for Religious Liberty

A Pastor Stephen Grant Novel

Ray Keating

This book is a work of fiction. Names, characters, places, events and incidents either are the product of the author's imagination or are used fictitiously. Any resemblance to actual persons, living or dead, events or locales is entirely coincidental.

For more information:
Keating Reports, LLC
P.O. Box 596
Manorville, NY 11949
keatingreports@aol.com

ISBN-10: 1480174491
ISBN-13: 978-1480174498

For
David,
Jonathan
and
Beth

Previous Books by Ray Keating

Root of All Evil? A Pastor Stephen Grant Novel (2012)

Warrior Monk: A Pastor Stephen Grant Novel (2010)

Discussion Guide for Warrior Monk: A Pastor Stephen Grant Novel (2011)

In the nonfiction arena...

"Chuck" vs. the Business World: Business Tips on TV (2011)

U.S. by the Numbers: What's Left, Right, and Wrong with America State by State (2000)

New York by the Numbers: State and City in Perpetual Crisis (1997)

D.C. by the Numbers: A State of Failure (1995)

“Behold, the virgin shall conceive and bear a son, and shall call his name Immanuel.”

- Isaiah 7:14

“A prison cell, in which one waits, hopes, does various unessential things, and is completely dependent on the fact that the door of freedom has to be opened *from the outside*, is not a bad picture of Advent.”

- Dietrich Bonhoeffer

“If the world hates you, know that it has hated me before it hated you. If you were of the world, the world would love you as its own; but because you are not of the world, but I chose you out of the world, therefore the world hates you. Remember the word that I said to you: A servant is not greater than his master. If they persecuted me, they will also persecute you.”

- John 15:18-20

“Congress shall make no law respecting an establishment of religion, or prohibiting the free exercise thereof...”

- First Amendment to the
U.S. Constitution

Prologue

The Grand Ballroom of the Waldorf Astoria on Park Avenue crackled with the energy of political euphoria.

Supporters of Adam Pritchett were celebrating what appeared to be a victory of historic proportions in the New York City mayoral race. Expensive champagne flowed among the two-thousand-plus revelers in the elegant four-story, two-tiered room. Money wasn't really an issue for Pritchett, and by extension, for his campaign. Nothing could derail what had come to be known as the "Pritchett Juggernaut."

Or, at least, that's how it seemed to everyone in the room, including campaign staff, donors, volunteers, Democratic Party officials, and even the media.

Pritchett ran one of the most unorthodox and expensive mayoral campaigns in New York's history – and that was saying something. He spent a prodigious amount of dollars on all kinds of political advertising, including television, radio, Internet and social media, newspapers and magazines, direct mail, billboards and seemingly every other paid advertising outlet.

At the same time, Pritchett completely ignored the media. He failed to do even one interview during the race, did not hold any press conferences, refused to participate in debates, and ignored questions shouted by reporters at campaign stops.

Pritchett, whose net worth topped the $280 million mark, built his wealth as one of New York's leading commercial real estate developers. The man's confidence in his own abilities was legendary in New York business circles, and when he decided to jump into politics by running for mayor, his arrogance only seemed to grow. Pritchett simply hired the best political advertising people in the nation, brought on a few political consultants willing to carry out his wishes with few questions, and saturated the largest and most expensive media market in the nation, perhaps the world, with his message.

That message was simple. Pritchett would bring crime, which had spiked over the past couple of years, back under control. He pledged to make sure that every city government job and program was protected, and the budget for public schools would rise. He was more than willing to jack up taxes on "my fellow wealthy residents who receive so much from this great city."

The unions loved him, as did the rest of the Democratic Party. After all, what wasn't there to love in a place like New York City? Pritchett was willing to spend his own money to get elected, and spend other people's money to expand government and fight crime, all while hiking taxes on the rich, of which he was a member. He was a liberal dream.

Pritchett's opponent didn't stand a chance.

The polls had closed a mere twenty minutes ago. The crushed Republican, Robert Nesci, already finished his concession speech. Now, the Pritchett faithful drank, danced and chanted their man's name. They grew ever more excited, with anticipation mounting for Pritchett's victory speech.

The only group in the room uniformly unenthused was the media. Despite the fact that they overwhelmingly subscribed to the same party affiliation and policy ideas as Pritchett, these reporters and commentators uniformly hated the guy for his arrogance and, more importantly, his cutting the media out of his campaign. It didn't matter if they agreed with his agenda or not, access denied was unacceptable. But they looked beaten, resigned to being on the outside looking in for the coming four years.

Just outside the ballroom, Pritchett buttoned his dark blue suit jacket, looked at a key aide, Maureen Donahue, and said, "Well, Maureen, ready to make history?"

She responded, "You've already done that, sir."

"You're right. But let's go make some more."

Donahue spoke into a cellphone. "Mayor-elect Pritchett is ready. He will be entering in a few seconds." The 30-year-old Donahue had a soothing voice, bright blue eyes, round face, easy smile, and shoulder length blond hair that combined in a way so that people seemed to automatically like her, and were willing to get things done for her.

Donahue waited about ten seconds, and then pointed to and smiled at a member of Pritchett's security team, signaling him to open the doors.

The security team formed a wedge in front of Pritchett, with Donahue and two other campaign officials trailing behind.

As Frank Sinatra belted out "New York, New York" amidst applause and shouts of approval, a spotlight focused on the smiling, waving Adam Pritchett. He didn't look the part of a powerful politician, nor business tycoon, for that matter. Pritchett was short and thin with messy, grayish hair, a pointed, pinched nose, and a nasally voice. He wore thick, square glasses, and somehow, his expensive, tailored suits never seemed to hang right on his body. The entire package combined to make him appear older than his 52 years.

At the podium, Pritchett eventually calmed the faithful long enough to begin his speech. Beyond the generic thank you to voters, his campaign staff and volunteers,

Pritchett's comments were noteworthy for their lack of generosity toward anyone.

While acknowledging his opponent's concession speech, Pritchett took a moment to point out, once more, just how wrong Nesci had been on the issues. There also was no use of the word "we" when talking about the campaign or his upcoming administration. Instead, it was "I" and "me."

But few of Pritchett's supporters seemed to notice or care.

Then he came to crime. Pritchett said, "And make no mistake, I will make sure that our city is retaken from criminals, that every man, woman and child, every resident, commuter and visitor, will again be safe in this leading global city."

The crowd erupted once more. A chant of "Pritchett, Pritchett" began and grew ever louder.

After nearly a minute, Pritchett lowered the volume of the crowd.

He began to speak again. "So, as your mayor…"

But a woman's voice rang out from the floor in front of Pritchett's podium. She yelled, "God bless you, Adam. We're praying for you!"

While many in the room responded with hoots of approval, Pritchett's face instantly transformed from victorious joy to controlled anger.

He pointed in the direction from where the call for blessings and prayers came, and said, "No! No, thank you. I don't want prayers. I don't want any god's blessing. I don't need it, and New York City certainly does not need it. And let's be clear, New York does not need religion in the public arena. So, save any talk of prayer for the pews and your private lives. Let's move away from such nonsense, and get back to the real world and real issues."

Several individuals cheered Pritchett's comments, including enthusiastic clapping from two of his three top campaign aides. Some of the Pritchett faithful halfheartedly applauded. But many in the room seemed bewildered, not sure how to react. That included Maureen Donahue.

- demonizing
- Anti-Christ
- too much detail
- boggs you down
- pushing too hard for conservatism

Chapter 1

The start of Pastor Stephen Grant's typical day had changed from his time years ago with the CIA.

As in the past, he did rise early and work out. But now, his morning exercises were shorter and less intense, and joined by prayer.

Grant still reviewed his schedule in his head while showering. Of course, the daily calendar for the pastor of St. Mary's Lutheran Church on the eastern end of Long Island was substantially different from a CIA analyst – his former official title – who possessed special skills learned as a Navy SEAL and further honed with the agency.

The most dramatic change was that other people were now involved in Grant's mornings. During his time with the CIA, Grant usually woke up and ate breakfast alone.

Today, his eyes opened to see his wife, Jennifer, lying next to him. Rather than jumping out of bed immediately, Stephen paused to appreciate her thin, fit body, sharp facial features, a slightly upturned nose, and dark auburn hair. On some mornings, Grant would be treated to a peek at her brown eyes and a smile, before she tried to grab a bit more sleep.

As for breakfast, when Jennifer wasn't traveling for her work as an economist, she and Stephen would have something quick and healthy on four mornings of the week.

On the other three days – Mondays, Wednesdays and Fridays – Grant typically would meet his two closest friends at the Moriches Bay Diner for devotions and discussion.

That was the case this Wednesday morning. Grant sat in a booth with Father Tom Stone, the Anglican rector at St. Bartholomew's Church, and Father Ron McDermott, from St. Luke's Roman Catholic Church and School.

With meetings, visits, Bible studies and other church-related activities scheduled throughout the rest of their respective days, each one – Stephen, six feet, black hair, green eyes and fit; Tom, gray hair and a bit overweight; and Ron, short, solid build and tightly cut blond hair – was dressed in the traditional black clerical garb, with a white square carved out of the collar.

They ordered breakfast, read from their preferred daily devotional – *For All the Saints: A Prayer Book For and By the Church* – and over eggs, bacon, oatmeal, a bagel, toast, orange juice, coffee and Diet Coke, discussed a few things going on in their lives and churches, from the mundane to the significant.

Ron, who was eating the oatmeal, said, "So, what do you make of this guy elected mayor in the city yesterday? The news this morning seems split on his huge margin of victory, and his stupid-ass comments on religion."

Tom replied, "An atheist winning big for mayor of New York City? Not exactly surprising territory."

"But based on his, as Ron put it, stupid-ass comments last night, he's more than just an atheist," commented Stephen.

"True," said Tom, who was piling bacon and scrambled eggs on a piece of toast. "He's a militant atheist."

Stephen agreed. "Throw in the mix that he's angry and apparently volatile. How else can you describe someone who reacts that way to having prayers said for him? I've dealt with some politicians over the years, as has Jennifer, and neither of us could think of another responding that way."

"How did he ever get elected?" asked Tom. "I thought almost every politician said 'God bless America' when done speaking."

"Not any more, apparently," answered Ron. "I was following this race a bit. He wouldn't speak to the media, or even debate his opponent. Instead, he completely controlled his message through massive media buys."

Tom added, "Maggie did mention the off-the-charts media purchases." Tom's wife, Maggie, ran her own public relations firm. "Do you guys think this was a passing gaffe, or something more?"

After swallowing a bite of his cinnamon-raisin bagel with cream cheese, Stephen said, "I looked at what he said online later in the night, and this clearly was more than a slip of the tongue. And it certainly wasn't just about his personal beliefs. He used specific and loaded language about New York City not needing religion in the public arena, and leaving prayer in the pews and in private lives."

Ron added, "Pritchett falls into the camp that wants to push religion out of the public square. The question is: How far does he take these views in terms of the law and policy?"

"It's not like we haven't seen similar efforts before," said Stephen, "and at higher levels of government than city mayor."

"But even in a lefty city like New York, how far could he go?" asked Tom.

Ron smirked. "You're kidding, right? Use your imagination. Just look at how far the effort has gone in redefining marriage in this state and others. And what about national political leaders, media like *The New York Times*, and television and cable networks aggressively pushing an agenda that undermines Judeo-Christian values? And federal policymakers forcing Christian churches to go against basic teachings? Religious liberty is under assault, my friend."

"Okay, you're right," admitted Tom somewhat sheepishly, though most of his attention seemed to be on eggs, bacon and toast.

Stephen said, "Unfortunately, it would not surprise me if this got a lot worse with Pritchett. He just strikes me as incredibly arrogant."

"On that uplifting note," said Tom, "let's shift topics to Thanksgiving and Advent. We're still set for you guys coming over for Thanksgiving, along with Zack, of course?"

Zackary Charmichael was a fairly recent arrival as the assistant pastor at St. Mary's.

Ron and Stephen nodded in the affirmative.

Tom also said, "And you're both ready for the Stone Bowl."

The nods continued.

Stephen added, "Don't forget that Jennifer is making her cinnamon crumb cake."

"Fabulous," acknowledged Tom.

Ron said, "While on the subject of the holidays, I just want to make sure that St. Bart's and St. Mary's are both set for the first Saturday in Advent for the ceremony setting up the community Nativity scene at St. Luke's?"

Tom rolled his eyes. "How many times are you going to ask this? Yes, we're both set. Both of our choirs will be there."

"Including our bell choir," said Stephen. "Relax, Ron, it'll go fine."

Chapter 2

After a brief hesitation, Maureen Donahue accepted Mayor-elect Pritchett's offer to become his press secretary for the transition team and for the Pritchett administration when it took office on January 1.

She clearly was pleased when Pritchett said, "Maureen, now that the campaign is over, I'm going to be communicating with the media more directly." He added, "Let's call a press conference for this coming Monday. I'll be announcing my first appointments."

So, less than a week after his historic victory, Mayor-elect Adam Pritchett stood before a throng of television, newspaper, Internet, radio and magazine reporters in the lobby of the audacious Pritchett Building on Fifth Avenue in midtown Manhattan.

Pritchett introduced three of his five deputy mayors, and his chief policy advisor.

Pritchett's selection to be deputy mayor for economic development was Dean Havenport. He had been with Pritchett for many years as the city government liaison with Pritchett NYC Enterprises, Inc. Another longtime employee and close advisor on political and personal donations, Carter Dujas, was made Pritchett's chief policy advisor.

But once the floor was opened to questions from the press, which had never happened before with Pritchett, it was all about his campaign night declarations on religion and the public life of the city.

Pritchett did not seem to be overly bothered by the questions, but he attempted several times to bring the focus back to his appointments. The press, sensing an opportunity to hurt this politician who ignored them throughout his run for office, failed to relent.

A *New York Post* columnist inquired, "Mayor-elect Pritchett, didn't your comments on Election Night, in effect, tell people of faith to take a hike, that there was no place for them in your administration or even in the life of New York City?"

The controlled anger seen on the previous Tuesday night reappeared on Pritchett's face. "Okay, if this is how it's going to go, fine. My comments on Tuesday night were not meant to exclude anyone from my effort to turn this city around, or to exclude anyone from contributing positively to the energy and life of our city. What it was meant to do was make clear that religion should not be a part of those efforts and should not be in the public life of our city in general. I believe in a very strict separation of church and state, and have seen little of value come out of religion. If you believe in some Supreme Being or force, that's your business. You obviously have that right, but keep it as your private business. There's no justification for it to be in our political and public lives."

That generated tremendous buzz among the assembled press corps, whose hands shot in the air, with many members calling out Pritchett's name and title to get his attention. Standing behind Pritchett, Havenport looked non-phased, even uninterested, in the current flurry of activity. Meanwhile, Dujas positively beamed. As for Donahue, she couldn't hide her discomfort.

Pritchett faced the shouts, flashes and cameras with his anger replaced by a calm delight. He was even smiling as he selected a *New York Times* reporter.

She asked, "Mayor-elect Pritchett, what about religious groups involved in helping to provide various social services, help for the homeless, education, and health care to those in need in the city?"

Pritchett replied, "To the extent that those services are supplied in partnership with city government, or if city funds are involved, those efforts will be re-evaluated by my administration."

That declaration created an even louder response among the media, and a bigger smile from Carter Dujas.

Chapter 3

Reverend Lee Morrison wasn't a real reverend in any true sense of the word. But he claimed the title a few years ago, and the 18 followers – ten men, five women and three children – who lived with him on 40 secluded, mountainous acres in the middle of Pennsylvania addressed Morrison as "Reverend."

The 39-year-old Morrison had been a volatile person since his early high school years. He was pushed along to get a diploma, and had no interest in attaining, nor the skills to earn, a college degree. But Morrison desperately wanted to join the military. The U.S. Army knew enough not to accept him, as did the Air Force, Navy and Marines when he gave each a try.

Morrison also exhibited a passionate fire at a small Baptist Church while growing up. But starting in Morrison's teen years, the church's pastor struggled to keep the young man focused on Jesus and what the Bible said, as opposed to what Lee Morrison was telling his fellow teenagers. In subsequent years, delusions about his own skills and greatness grew, and transformed into his espousing that he had become God's general in battling evil in America.

The small church was being ripped apart by Morrison, so he finally was forced to leave. Several families followed him to his current compound. But many later wandered away when paramilitary training was integrated into daily life, and Morrison grew still more strident and extreme.

A few years ago, the only disciples left with Morrison were the current 15 people, including four married couples, with three young children among them. All of the adults were social outcasts, feeling that no one beyond their small circle understood who they were and what they were trying to accomplish. Morrison gave them a sense of purpose, that they were part of something bigger. They proclaimed that Morrison was a leader, a man worth following, a prophet of God. For all but one of the followers, it meant doing anything for the Reverend, because it meant doing anything for God. Even that remaining disciple would have done almost anything.

Morrison had just watched the soon-to-be-mayor of New York City. He shut the television off in a fit of frustration. "Godless bastard!" Morrison walked across the room in a large log home to a desk with an intercom system. He hit two buttons, and spoke into a microphone. "Brothers and sisters, please report to the gathering room in the main building, immediately." He repeated the message, which was carried over speaker systems across the six buildings located on the group's grounds.

Ten minutes later, Morrison described what he had just seen on television. He proclaimed, "This is a call to action from above. This is an attack on 'One nation under God.' New York long has been a cesspool of sin and atheism. Everyone knows that. But now, this Pritchett has gone too far. He must be stopped! And brothers and sisters, we're the people that God has chosen to stop him before he actually becomes mayor of New York. We must begin planning and training. Rejoice, my brothers and sisters, we are the chosen soldiers of Jesus. Hallelujah and amen!"

Fourteen followers echoed their leader's hallelujah and amen. One did not.

As people left to go about their tasks, Eli Cranston asked to speak to Morrison alone.

Cranston sat across an oak desk from Morrison, and said, "Can I ask you a favor, sir?"

The two men were starkly different. Cranston was a bit gaunt and tall, with disheveled light brown hair and a beard. Meanwhile, Morrison was muscular, short, and had long brown hair. But it was more than their appearances. Morrison radiated confidence, while Cranston was nervous and unsure.

"Of course, Eli, what can I do for you, brother?"

"I'd like to leave."

"Really, why?"

"I've been thinking some about reconnecting with my family. My brother, his wife and kids live in Georgia."

"I see. Is there anything more, anything bothering you?"

"Well, I don't want to be dishonest with you, Reverend."

"Yes?"

Eli scratched his beard. "I'm not comfortable with targeting that new mayor of New York. I agree that he is doing the devil's work. But I can't be involved in killing him. I cannot do that. I'm not strong enough."

Cranston avoided looking into Morrison's dark eyes.

Morrison's voice was soothing. "Very well, Eli. I understand. God has different plans for each of us."

Relief washed over Cranston's face. "Thank you, so much, sir."

Morrison added, "When do you plan on leaving, my brother?"

"I'm anxious to see my family, so I was thinking about heading out this afternoon."

"So soon?"

"If that's alright, I thought I would hike into town, and head to the bus station?"

"Of course, but no hiking. I'll drive you into town. Besides, I have to grab some supplies. Could you be ready in a couple of hours?"

"I'll go get ready. Again, thank you, Reverend, and God bless."

"And God bless you, Eli."

Just over two hours later, Morrison guided a large, beat up pickup truck down the rough, mountain road. Cranston sat next to him, clutching a duffle bag.

Morrison braked and turned down a smaller, even rougher road.

Cranston asked, "Why are we turning, Reverend?"

"Just need to do one thing before heading into town."

After traveling a quarter mile down the road, Morrison stopped, and shut off the vehicle.

The nervous Cranston asked, "What are we doing, Reverend?"

Morrison reached across the cab and opened the glove compartment in front of Cranston. He grabbed the 9mm Colt Defender pistol that was inside.

"Oh, God, what are you doing, sir?"

"The Lord's work, Eli, and I can't risk you placing that work in peril. Get out."

Morrison directed Cranston to the edge of a small pit. He said, "Eli, throw your duffle bag down there, please."

Cranston did so, and then pleaded, "You can't do this. Is this what God wants?"

Morrison replied, "Apparently, it is. Like I said, there are different plans for each of us."

Morrison fired two bullets.

He grabbed a shovel from the back of the truck, and tossed a combination of soil and leaves on top of the body of Eli Cranston and his duffle bag.

Then Morrison drove into town for supplies.

Chapter 4

The intercom buzzed on the cherry wood desk of Francis Cardinal Capriano, Archbishop of New York. His secretary announced, "Your Eminence, Mayor-elect Pritchett is on Line 1."

Cardinal Capriano took a deep breath. "Thank you, Kathleen."

He picked up the phone, and hit the button next to the blinking light. "Mayor-elect Pritchett, thanks very much for calling back, and congratulations on your big win at the polls."

"That's very kind, Cardinal Capriano. What is it that you wished to talk about?"

"Well, I'm sure you can understand how anxious many of us in the Catholic community were about your remarks at the press conference yesterday regarding the work the church does with and for this great city that we both love so much. The New York Archdiocese and various Catholic institutions have long worked together with the city to help the weakest among us. I just wanted to make sure that this beneficial relationship will continue under your administration."

"I can't say that."

Capriano stood up from his desk. "I'm sorry, but what does that mean, Mayor-elect Pritchett?"

"I'm not willing to make any announcements just yet."

"With all due respect, Mr. Pritchett, do you realize how much the Catholic Church, as well as other religious institutions, do for the people of this city? I hope you are not seriously going to place that critical work at risk? I realize that we differ in our views on religion, but ..."

Pritchett interrupted. "Cardinal Capriano, I returned your call out of courtesy because of past relationships between your church and the city. But that's the last such courtesy you will be getting from my administration. Yes, I intend to bring this church-city relationship to an end. I've heard many talk about all of the good you do for people. Quite frankly, though, I see nothing that you do that cannot be done by other private, non-religious organizations, or by the city itself, and done far better. All that I have ever seen from you people is bigotry, discrimination, superstition, judgment, divisiveness and hate. There's no place for that in my city. Good day, sir."

Pritchett hung up.

Cardinal Capriano sat down in his chair, his mouth and eyes wide open, and phone still in his ear. After a few more seconds, he slowly hung up the phone.

The Cardinal leaned back in his chair, and looked at the crucifix hanging on the wall across the room from his desk. "Dear Lord, we need your help. The Holy Spirit has a lot of work to do." He paused. "What are we going to do with this jack ass?"

Chapter 5

After hanging up with Cardinal Capriano, Adam Pritchett got up from his black, shiny, U-shaped desk. He paced around his large office, located on the 19th floor of the Pritchett Building. He stopped at the floor-to-ceiling windows, and looked down on the traffic creeping along Fifth Avenue.

"Presumptuous, son-of-a-bitch Cardinal," he muttered.

Pritchett walked over and swung open his office door.

He barked at his assistant. "Erin, tell Donahue to be in my office in an hour. In the meantime, no calls, no disturbances."

Before Erin could reply, Pritchett slammed the door shut.

He began typing at one of the computers on his desk.

Sixty minutes later, Maureen Donahue knocked at his door.

"Come in, Maureen," called Pritchett.

"Good afternoon, sir. What can I do for you?"

Pritchett pulled a sheet of paper off the printer in the corner of his office. "Sit down."

He sat inside the U, and reached across the top of the desk, handing Donahue the paper. "I need you to edit this, and then get it out to the press immediately. I've already sent it to your inbox."

As she started to read, her shoulders slumped slightly.

"Is there something that you want to say, Maureen?"

She continued reading. "Um, no. Well, have you run this by the transition team, or anyone else?"

His eyes narrowed behind the thick, square glasses. "Of course not. Why should I? They work for me, and are paid nicely to do what I tell them to do. As is the case with you."

"Yes, yes, of course, Mr. ... I mean, Mayor-elect Pritchett. I'll have a final copy for your approval in a half hour." She could not fully hide the disappointment in her voice.

"Good." Pritchett turned to the next task on his desk.

Donahue got up and slowly left the room, while re-reading the statement that Pritchett had written. It was short and direct, and inflammatory.

When she got back to her own office, she called Dean Havenport. Donahue read him the statement, and made clear her strong reservations.

But Havenport was unconcerned. He said, "Don't worry about it, Maureen. This is who Adam is. He's set on this, and you won't be able to derail him. Just do what he told you to do."

Donahue tried calling her parents. But she only got a recording to leave a message. She didn't bother, and hung up. Maureen woke up her desktop, and pulled the document up on her screen.

It was an announcement from the Mayor-elect that one of the first duties of his staff after taking office would be to compile information on all religious institutions and groups receiving funding from and/or partnering with city government, with the intent to begin phasing out such "inappropriate relationships."

Pritchett was quoted in the release declaring, "While I presume that the past work of various religious groups is appreciated by many New Yorkers, these efforts clearly violate the separation of church and state, and need to be phased down and eventually eliminated. But my fellow

New Yorkers need not worry. Other private, non-religious organizations and, of course, our city government can pick up all of these tasks. In fact, I have no doubt that we will carry out these responsibilities far more efficiently and professionally than they have been done before. While people are, of course, free to worship or not worship as they see fit in their private lives, religion need not, and should not, be a part of New York City's public life."

Chapter 6

The political reaction to Mayor-elect Adam Pritchett's statement was swift and massive.

Republicans, of course, pounced.

The press secretary for the Republican White House said, "The President is very concerned about this disturbing attempt to push God out of the public square. He said, and I quote, 'The Constitution guarantees freedom of religion, and that means people of faith are free to bring their beliefs into the public arena to weigh in on the issues of our day, and to help their fellow Americans. Government should not be looking to suppress our freedoms, but instead is here to protect our God-given rights.'"

Sal Antonio, a Republican state senator from Staten Island, simply declared, "This guy and his anti-religion crusade make me freakin' sick. I wanted to puke listening to him. God help us and this city for the next four years with him as mayor."

For good measure, Robert Nesci, Pritchett's GOP opponent in the race for mayor, said, "Pritchett's out of control, and he is going to make New York City a national battleground over the issue of religious liberty."

Meanwhile, the Democrats appeared split. A small group of state representatives and city council members took to the steps of City Hall to defend Pritchett. As he approached the microphones, State Assemblyman Blair

Quinton brushed back his blond hair, buttoned his expensive charcoal-colored suit, and adjusted the Rolex on his wrist. He said, "I heartily endorse what Mayor-elect Pritchett is doing. He is absolutely correct to undertake this review and reassessment of religious groups involved in city matters. I've long wondered why city government would be working with churches, especially the Catholic Church, that stand against so much of what we have achieved in this city in terms of expanding the rights of women, and the gay, lesbian and transgendered communities."

But many Democrats in city and state government seemed taken off guard by Pritchett's actions. They were bewildered as to how to proceed. That is, except for City Councilman Marvin Sanders.

In addition to being on the city council, Sanders was a pastor at the Agape A.M.E. Church in Brooklyn. After Quinton's group finished making statements and answering questions, he stepped up and unreservedly mixed politics and religion. Sanders was a short, thin black man, but with a deep, powerful voice. He declared, "I am filled with righteous anger. I campaigned for Mr. Pritchett. I believed that he would improve safety in this city, while also protecting many vital programs. But now, he has declared war on churches helping to do the Lord's work in New York. My God, why? I am distressed. I am outraged. I am saddened. If he succeeds in this bizarre pursuit, it is, of course, the most vulnerable who will suffer, including children and single mothers. I will work hard, with every fiber of my being, to stop Mayor-elect Pritchett's misguided plan, while also praying just as hard that he will come to see and understand all of the good that churches and other religious groups do in this city. None of us are beyond forgiveness and redemption thanks to our Lord and Savior, Jesus Christ."

Chapter 7

The purely religious reaction in the New York City area to Mayor-elect Pritchett's statement included confusion, puzzlement, indignation, calls for prayer, fury and even some panic.

Many of the confused could be found on the theological Left. Bishop Barney Flanders, of the Episcopal Church's New York diocese, was quoted in a local paper saying, "I'm just shocked. The Episcopal Church long has been a voice for the social gospel, open to change, loving all and certainly not judging anyone. We have a distinguished history of working with the city to aid the poor. I'm hoping that Mayor-elect Pritchett was not thinking about us when talking about excluding religion from the public square. After all, we are a voice of reason."

Leaving his offices, Pritchett was asked about Bishop Flanders' comment. He laughed and said, "Reason and religion are incompatible. It does not matter whether a religious group is considered liberal or conservative, this will be a comprehensive policy that does not differentiate."

The director of the largest Catholic social services provider observed, "If Mayor-elect Pritchett carries through on this idea, it will devastate our budget and our work."

In response to that observation, one conservative Catholic commentator said, "Pritchett is out to lunch. His atheism is the most radical of any elected official I've come across. At the same time, maybe this incident will serve as a wake up call to Catholic and other religious charitable endeavors as to the dangers of taking handouts from the government."

Dr. Brett Matthews, president of the Lutheran Church-Missouri Synod's Atlantic District, told a reporter, "I'm deeply saddened by the path chosen by Mayor-elect Pritchett. Unfortunately, I think his extremist take on religion is not all that uncommon today. We all must pray for him, for this city, and for God to help us heal a culture torn apart by sin."

Finally, Keith Diehl, pastor of the independent Ark of Righteousness Church in Jamaica, Queens, simply proclaimed, "Adam Pritchett is a tool of Satan. There is no other explanation."

Chapter 8

Stephen was putting the finishing touches on a simple, tasty breakfast of Cream of Wheat mixed with macadamia nuts, banana and brown sugar.

Meanwhile, after pouring two tall glasses of orange juice, Jennifer had the Thursday *Wall Street Journal* spread out on the island bar in the middle of their kitchen. She was reading the New York section. "The backlash against Pritchett is amazing, and it just keeps mounting."

Stephen brought two bowls of his Cream of Wheat creation over, and placed one in front of Jennifer. He observed, "Pritchett deserves it."

Jennifer put the newspaper down, and looked at the bowl. "Cream of Wheat? I can't believe that's what you made."

Stephen said, "Why the skepticism?"

"I don't know. Cream of Wheat? It always sounded like something you had as a kid, a long time ago. Even before you were a child."

"Funny. Try it."

Jennifer captured two pieces of macadamia and some banana on the spoon, and gave it a try. She let it move around her mouth a bit, chewed and swallowed.

Stephen asked, "Well?"

She smiled. "Okay, you won me over."

"I thought so." Stephen consumed a large spoonful.

As she ate, Jennifer returned to the *Journal*. This was part of her morning ritual. But the focus this time was not on the latest bit of economic data, some change in tax policy, or one of the paper's spot-on editorials. It was, again, Mayor-elect Pritchett.

She observed, "It's rather amazing. He just does not seem to care what the fallout is. Given the way he ran his campaign, perhaps that's not so surprising. He listened to no one else during the campaign, ran it the way he wanted. And now, apparently, that's how he's going to govern. On a certain level, that's admirable."

"Admirable?" Stephen blurted out with Cream of Wheat and banana in his mouth.

"I obviously don't agree with this attack on religion. In fact, I don't agree with him on much of anything. But his willingness to do what he wants, and damn the torpedoes, does have a certain admirable aspect to it. I wish more of the conservative elected officials I agree with exhibited a bit of that."

Stephen replied, "You have a point. Many in the Church could use a bit more damn-the-torpedoes attitude on occasion. In fact, some of that's going to be needed in responding to Pritchett. This is a critical time when Christians need to come together, and join with other religious leaders, to counter this Pritchett assault."

"Are you going to address it in your sermon this weekend?"

"Absolutely. I have to do a closer review of this weekend's readings, and see how this Pritchett mess can tie in. It's important to make clear that the Church has a responsibility to weigh in on issues where Scripture speaks clearly. And this is another outrageous case of government attacking our religious liberties."

Jennifer smiled. "A little passionate? Sounds like you've got a good chunk of that sermon already written in your head."

Chapter 9

Carter Dujas possessed the ideal resume to serve as chief policy advisor for the soon-to-be mayor of New York City. He earned an undergraduate degree in political science from University of California, Berkeley, and a master's degree in public policy from the Harvard Kennedy School.

But there was much more, of course. Dujas and Pritchett were unified not only in their political views, but also in an atheism that had no tolerance for religion of any kind.

The actions of Adam Pritchett since winning election in no way surprised Carter Dujas. Rather, Dujas enthusiastically supported what Pritchett was saying and doing.

Dujas sat across the desk from Pritchett in the 19th floor office. Their similar thinking was not reflected in their physical appearances. Not only was he fifteen years younger, but unlike Pritchett, Dujas' brown suit fit well, his blond hair was neatly cut, and his facial features were rounder and softer.

"What do you have, Carter?" asked Pritchett in a typically demanding, nasally tone.

"Well, Adam, I just got an e-mail from Perry. They've finally decided to take a big step in this year's report, and add the Roman Catholic Church to the list of hate groups in the U.S."

"Really? It's about damn time."

"Yes, but Perry wants to know if you're okay with doing so right now, given your election as mayor."

"What does he mean?"

"I believe he wants to know if you want the group to hold off on adding the Catholic Church to the list until after you leave office. Perry wrote that he would understand if that was the case."

Perry Harris was the president of a self-proclaimed watchdog group called Atheists for a Caring World. Part of the ACW's mission was to bring attention to good deeds done by atheists, and to provide articles and studies showing that atheists were more humane than religious people. But most notably, and notoriously, the group produced an annual report listing so-called "hate" groups across the nation. That report was first published three years earlier. But beyond a few easy picks, like various white supremacist organizations, the remaining list featured socially conservative groups, along with some pastors and independent Christian churches that usually were very vocal and less-than-loving in their declarations on sin and sinners. In the end, the ACW "hate" groups list overwhelmingly was a list of organizations that ACW supporters disagreed with on hot-button social issues.

More than 60 percent of ACW's budget came from Adam Pritchett. In fact, the entire effort was the brainchild of Pritchett and Dujas, who hired Harris, a friend from Berkeley, to set the entire thing up.

As was his ritual when making a decision, Pritchett rose from his chair and walked over to the large windows over Fifth Avenue. "I have no doubt that most people would advise me to tell Perry to wait. They're worried that I've done too much already to stir up churches and other religious wackos."

Dujas said, "I think it's safe to say that almost everyone in the political world, including our fellow Democrats, would say let it go, at least until after you're done being mayor."

Pritchett was still staring out the window. "True. And what do you think I should do, Carter?"

"Adam, you know what I think. When done as mayor, you lose the soapbox of being mayor. And it's always better to strike immediately than at some vague time in the future."

"You're right. Tell Perry, it's a go. In fact, tell him to release the report tomorrow morning."

Dujas smiled. "Consider it done."

Pritchett added, "By the way, let's keep in mind that over the next couple of years, ACW should add other Christian churches. And during my second term as mayor, then we'll add some of those conservative and Orthodox Jews."

Dujas replied, "Looking forward to it."

Chapter 10

Maureen Donahue was summoned to Pritchett's office before 8:00 AM on Friday morning.

Once again, her boss handed her a sheet of paper with a statement he had typed up. His order was to read it, edit it, and get a final version back to him before nine.

As she read, Donahue's face was transformed from curiosity to incredulity. But then her expression signaled resignation, which then turned to the most rare of displays by Maureen Donahue – anger.

She turned on her employer. "What's wrong with you?"

"Excuse me, Ms. Donahue?"

"You heard me. Are you intent on committing political suicide?"

The volume of Pritchett's voice grew louder. "Listen here, Donahue..."

But Donahue's voice went still louder, and carried a nervous energy. "No, you listen, Mr. Pritchett. You need to hear this. Agreeing with some fringe group classifying the Catholic Church as a hate group. That's insane."

"Ms. Donahue, I not only agree with this assessment, but I fund the group that publishes this study."

"You do what?"

"You heard me."

Donahue took a deep breath, stood up, and returned the sheet of paper to Pritchett's desk. She said, "Mayor-elect

Pritchett, throughout the campaign, I had questions about your temperament and decision making, but it all seemed to work out. It's apparent to me now, though, that you are the wrong person to be elected mayor, or for that matter, to be elected to any office. You have no interest in bringing this city together, but only in ripping it apart. And I've had enough of your anti-religion bigotry. I cannot in good conscience remain in your employ. I will clean out my office immediately."

She turned and left, making sure that her former employer could not see her shaking hands.

Pritchett watched her go, and then said out loud, "Pain in the ass. So damn inconvenient."

He pecked away at a keyboard, then picked up the phone. He hit Dujas' extension. "Carter. Donahue just quit. You're going to have to play press secretary until we get someone new. I just e-mailed you the statement for today. Get it ready by nine."

By 10:00 AM, the political, religious and media communities exploded in a frenzy of activity.

Chapter 11

His cellphone rang for the fourth time in the past hour. Assorted media were seeking comment on the decision by Atheists for a Caring World to classify the Catholic Church as a hate group, along with New York City Mayor-elect Adam Pritchett's strong statement in support.

Rollin Dawes, director of the Patriotic Atheists for America, expected some calls. Luckily, his schedule as a vice president of security for a San Francisco-based software company gave him some flexibility.

As an ex-Catholic, he was enthusiastic to speak about his former church being classified as a hate group. His younger brother had been abused by a priest as a teenager, and wound up committing suicide while Dawes was serving in Afghanistan.

Dawes blamed all Catholic clergy for his brother's death, and became convinced that God did not, could not, exist.

He became adamant in telling anyone who would listen that God was a hoax, and a cruel one, but also that atheists were patriots who loved their nation. That led to the creation of the small, but vocal, Patriotic Atheists for America. Few paid attention, until now.

Dawes told a local newspaper reporter, "I admire Adam Pritchett. He won election to become mayor of the nation's largest city, and he has stood firm in his atheism in the face of enormous pressure from political and religious leaders. Pritchett has bravely taken on the world's most powerful and dangerous entity, the Catholic Church. That church is well known for peddling superstition, brainwashing, and yes, hate. This is a man to be admired. We need more leaders like him in America. He is the type of man that I'd be willing to follow into battle, and in fact, will follow into this battle."

Other atheist and militant leftist groups chimed in with praise for the ACW's report and New York's Adam Pritchett.

Chapter 12

While he was watching the morning's developments on the small television in his office at St. Mary's Lutheran Church in Manorville, Pastor Stephen Grant just kept shaking his head.

Zack Charmichael, the assistant pastor at St. Mary's, sat on a couch next to Grant's armchair. Zack provided a running commentary to go along with what was being said on television.

Grant moved over to his desk, picked up the phone and called Father Ron McDermott at St. Luke's Catholic Church. The St. Luke's secretary patched Stephen through.

Ron immediately answered, "Can you believe this crap, Stephen?"

"Part of me is shocked, and part me knows that I shouldn't be surprised by anything any more in terms of these kinds of attacks and the attention they receive."

"I know what you mean. I can't decide who pisses me off more – the crackpot atheist group for labeling the church a hate group, the media for giving them credibility, or Pritchett for chiming in."

"Take a deep breath, Ron."

"Unfortunately, no time right now for long breaths. I've got to go. Have to dial in on a conference call in a few minutes."

"I understand. I'm praying, my friend."

"Thanks. We'll talk later."

Just after hanging up, the phone rang. Stephen called out, "Barb, I've got it."

"Thanks," replied Barbara, the seventy-plus-year-old, gray-haired church secretary.

Stephen said, "St. Mary's Lutheran Church."

"Stephen?"

"Yes, who is this?"

"It's Brett. Don't you have a church secretary and an assistant pastor, and yet, you're answering the phones?"

"I try not to let my massive staff go to my head. Answering the phones keeps me grounded. Are you taking in the Pritchett show?"

"Unfortunately, yes. That's why I am calling. Are you available for a conference call in an hour with Dr. Piepkorn, as well as Bruce Ericsson?"

Dr. Harrison Piepkorn was the president of the national Lutheran Church-Missouri Synod that Stephen and St. Mary's called home, and Bruce Ericsson was the pastor at St. John's Lutheran Cathedral in New York City.

Stephen replied, "Sure, what are we doing?"

"Well, that's what we're going to try to figure out."

Within the hour, Stephen was alone in his office, a room that was dominated by bookcases covering two walls and bordering a large window on a third. The fourth wall had a large, antique wardrobe positioned next to the door.

He leaned back in his comfortable, swivel chair, looking out the large bay window at the church parking lot. He started thinking and praying about what might lie ahead.

Thanksgiving next week. Christmas sales long in full swing. Even with so many troubles, we're so blessed in this country. So much to thank you for, Lord. But the Adam Pritchetts of the world do the exact opposite, not only trying to push You out of their own lives, but out of everyday life for all. And the Pritchetts no longer are the fringe. He's just ahead of the curve as to where radical relativism and secularism would take us. We need the Holy Spirit. It's almost Advent. We await. Please help. Amen.

Stephen checked the time. It was 12:59 PM. He punched in the conference call number, along with the access code. Two beeps, and he was in the call.

"Good afternoon, everyone," said Stephen to announce his arrival.

Greetings flowed back from the other three pastors – Piepkorn, Matthews and Ericsson.

Piepkorn began, "Thanks for taking a little time out of your day for this call. I think it's critical that we start thinking about how to respond to what this new mayor of New York is putting out there. Make no mistake, if the Catholic Church is deemed a so-called hate group, we and all other churches will soon be added to that list."

Stephen had come to know Dr. Piepkorn in recent times. Grant appreciated the man's commitment to Holy Scripture, his focus on expanding access to education at the church's two seminaries, and his loving but firm dealings with various factions within the denomination. Stephen also knew that this attack on Christians in the public arena struck at Piepkorn's goal of working more closely with other traditional Christian churches on issues where a clear, unified, public voice was needed.

Piepkorn continued, "Given that you guys are on the ground there, can you tell me anything more about Pritchett and his objectives?"

Matthews gave a rundown on the unique campaign that Pritchett ran. He added, "Beyond his business dealings, the man really was a mystery to most. I checked around once he spoke out during his victory speech, and no one that I'm in contact with in the larger Christian community in the metro area knew anything, and none of them were in contact with his campaign."

"So, this really was out of the blue?" asked Piepkorn, in a voice that held a slight Southern tinge reflecting his South Carolina roots.

Matthews replied, "Yes, unless Bruce or Stephen heard anything different?"

Bruce Ericsson was a mid-thirties pastor from rural North Dakota. His Nordic ancestry was unmistakable with blue eyes, a large build, and light blond hair that came down to his shirt collar. Anyone having seen hit superhero movies could not miss his resemblance to Thor, the god of thunder. His deep voice was rather thunder-ish as well. Ericsson had accepted the formidable challenge of revitalizing and making fiscally viable St. John's Lutheran Cathedral on Manhattan's upper west side, and was making slow progress.

Ericsson said, "Well, the only thing that I would note is that one parishioner mentioned to me in the summer that he discovered that Pritchett was a big funder and backer of radical atheists, and was frustrated with the media failing to get the word out. I didn't think anything of it at the time, since this guy comes off as a bit of a conspiracy nut. But apparently, at least this time, he was right."

Piepkorn said, "Thank you, Bruce. Stephen, anything on your end?"

"Sorry, but my knowledge of Pritchett was limited to what everyone else seemed to know. Nothing special."

Piepkorn said, "Okay. Now, the question is the response. If we don't answer this swiftly and clearly, I have no doubt that what Pritchett and his allies are trying will gain traction in other parts of the country."

Stephen said, "I agree. On too many issues in recent times, the Church in general has been content to speak timidly or even sit on the sidelines, when it should be speaking out with boldness and love, energized and protected by the Word of God. As a result, we've been put on the defensive, and now we have an extremist group labeling the Catholic Church as a hate group, a newly elected mayor of the nation's largest city agreeing and media coverage providing some degree of legitimacy."

Matthews added, "But what are the details of our response?"

Piepkorn said, "First, one of our church members from New Jersey has a very successful business, and is very frustrated. He contacted me this morning right after Pritchett made his latest announcement. He has pledged to make a very large donation to the church for a national television advertising buy that would serve as both a response to Pritchett and a call to join us."

"That's wonderful. God bless him," declared Matthews.

"Indeed. I've already assigned folks to getting this rolling. The second part of our response must come from our churches in New York City and the surrounding area."

Matthews volunteered, "Absolutely, Harrison. After this morning's escapades, I decided to contact Cardinal Capriano, and find out what their game plan is and see if we can get involved. I was going to contact him just as your office called me."

"That's ideal. I don't want to cut this call short, but it seems to me that you should immediately contact the Cardinal to scope out their response, and the possibilities of our involvement. Then, we can make an informed decision on how to proceed on the ground in New York. Does that make sense?"

Everyone else agreed.

Piepkorn concluded, "Thank you, gentlemen, for your service to our Lord and His Church. I am praying for you in this time of great challenge."

Chapter 13

It was just after 9:00 PM, but Cardinal Capriano finally was able to return the call of President Matthews.

The two men came to know each other as their paths crossed at various charity events. But they became friends after discovering a mutual passion for tennis. On occasion, they scheduled an early morning match. In addition, they shared a positive outlook on life evident from being quick to laugh and smile, and generally ranking as "people persons." When together, Capriano and Matthews also resembled clergy bookends, both average build, generally fit, and sporting shiny baldheads and silver, wire-rimmed glasses. The primary difference was Matthews having a gray beard and mustache, while Capriano was clean-shaven.

After exchanging standard pleasantries, Matthews commented, "Francis, how are things going? I saw your response to Pritchett on NBC. You struck the right tone, justified outrage and disgust, while also exhibiting love for your accusers. I don't know if I could be as measured and generous."

"It wasn't easy at all, Brett. The man is a jackass. But as you know, it's all about Chapter 10:19-20 in Matthew." After telling his disciples that they would face persecution, Jesus said, "When they deliver you over, do not be anxious how you are to speak or what you are to say, for what you are to say will be given to you in that hour. For it is not you who speak, but the Spirit of your Father speaking through you."

Matthews remarked, "Indeed. I called to see how we Lutherans can help?"

"This attack on the Catholic Church has generated an incredible outpouring from our Christian brethren, along with calls from Jewish, Muslim and other leaders and groups. It's been incredible."

"Well, at least, that's a blessing."

"It also got us seriously thinking about how we can work together. I've been in discussions most of the day with the Vatican and the U.S. Conference of Bishops. We've just put together the basics of a proposal that we plan on finalizing over the weekend, and announcing on Monday morning. That being the case, please don't share what I'm about to tell you, other than with your President Piepkorn and only the closest people you fully trust."

"Of course."

"Our announcement on Monday actually will be an invitation to fellow Christians to join us in what we're calling 'An Advent for Religious Liberty.' Specifically, in New York City, we're going to organize Christian prayer services nightly throughout Advent near the Christmas tree at Rockefeller Center, led by a different denomination or church each evening. We're hoping that similar gatherings will spring up more organically across the nation, and perhaps around the world."

"It's a perfect contrast to what Pritchett has been serving up. The late Pope Augustine also would have approved, I think."

Pope Augustine was known for his attempt to bring Christians together on common challenges, though his effort largely went dormant with his death.

"That occurred to me as well. Anyway, I'm especially concerned about the time frame. This all has to happen so fast, with Advent starting in about two weeks."

"Don't be surprised when this all comes together in a way that far exceeds anyone's expectations."

"From your lips to God's ears, Brett."

"Prayer, faith, and of course, hard work will make it happen. Count we Lutherans in, by the way. What do we need to do to help make this happen?"

These two men, despite differences on various issues of doctrine and interpretation of Scripture, spoke for another forty minutes, not as one Catholic priest and one Lutheran pastor, but as two Christians called and compelled in a unified mission to protect the Church of Jesus Christ, as well as the liberty of all to practice and speak out for their religion.

Chapter 14

Stephen Grant, Zack Charmichael, Ron McDermott and Tom Stone decided to try something new during the NFL season. Schedules permitting, the plan was to get together, along with family and friends, for Sunday Night Football.

It was supposed to be down time to enjoy each other's company, a few snacks, drinks, good discussion, and hopefully, an exciting game.

Ten weeks into the season, they'd only managed to gather five times, which was better than probably any of them expected, given their many activities.

It was Ron's turn to host. All four clergy members were in attendance, along with Tom's wife, Maggie, and Jennifer Grant.

St. Luke's rectory was a large, white Victorian, which sat across the parking lot from the church building and across the street from St. Luke's school. Everything in the house was big, from the staircase to the high ceilings to the expansive rooms.

Stephen's only regret with the games being at Ron's was the furniture. It was uncomfortable. Of course, he never mentioned this to anyone, not even Jennifer.

But when Ron's guests entered the living room in the back of the house, each looked stunned by the transformation.

The dull, cream-colored walls had been transformed by a light blue on two walls and yellow on the other two, and a 60-inch flat-screen television hung on the far wall above an entertainment center. A darker blue, deep, plush sectional couch, with two matching chairs, replaced the hard armchairs and sofa.

Zack was the first to enter, and proclaimed, "Ron, sweet."

Stephen followed and his mouth fell open. "Ron, this is great! When did you develop taste?"

"I'd been planning it for a while, and had it done this past week." The normally reserved Ron McDermott seemed a bit giddy. "I don't care what these three guys think. I want to know if it meets the approval of Jennifer and Maggie?"

Maggie Stone had a way of making people generally feel good. Her smile lit up an already bright face, with blue eyes framed by shoulder-length strawberry-blond hair. She declared, "Ron, I have to say, knowing you, this is a bold, unexpected step. It works very well. I love it."

Ron's smile grew, as he turned to Jennifer. "It's wonderful, Ron. The wall colors really enliven everything."

As Tom sank into the new couch, he sarcastically added, "Yes, Ron, I love the way the yellow pops. You've made quite a statement with your newfound decorating skills. Perhaps we should watch HGTV rather than the game tonight."

Maggie gave him a slap on the back of the head before she sat down next to him.

Stephen chimed in, "Ron, perhaps another time on the HGTV thing. We're not missing Bengals-Seahawks tonight."

"Darn straight," added Zack, who had claimed one of the new reclining chairs for his thin, five-foot-seven-inch body.

"Oh yes, we have the only two people in the state of New York who care about this game tonight," said Ron. "It's a battle of the St. Mary's pastors. Have you guys made a wager?"

Stephen grew up just outside Cincinnati, and Zack came from Seattle.

Stephen replied, "Absolutely."

Tom asked, "Care to share?"

Zack answered, "Loser covers the other guy's Confirmation classes for the month of January." He smiled, pushing his rectangular, brown-rimmed glasses up on his nose just a bit.

Ron whistled. "I like that. Dumping Confirmation on a football bet."

Stephen said, "Thanks for making it sound so unsavory."

Ron laughed. "No problem."

Tom added, "Zack seems to have the full team spirit with the Seahawks jersey. Why aren't you in Bengal regalia, Stephen?"

Jennifer cut in, "He's still moping about the Reds being knocked out of the playoffs early. The sulking has extended to football as well." Stephen was wearing a black polo shirt and jeans.

Ron noted, "Oh, right. How long is this going to go on, Stephen?"

"Until spring training, I would imagine," Stephen answered.

The food options were a varied presentation of cookies, nachos, pretzels, chips, dip, soda, coffee, beer and wine. Given it was a Sunday night in the clergy world, by halftime, the energy level in the room had fallen considerably, except for Zack, whose Seahawks had stretched out a two touchdown lead.

On the way back from the refrigerator, as he handed cold Heinekens to Zack and Ron, Tom moved the conversation off football. He asked Ron, "Hey, have you heard anything official from your bosses on the response to the Pritchett hate group thing?"

"Nothing official. Just rumors."

Stephen said, "Actually, I got a call early this evening from Dr. Matthews. He got the scoop from Cardinal Capriano on what will be announced tomorrow morning."

Ron smirked. "Why am I not surprised that you have better contacts with the Catholic Church hierarchy on this issue than my own?"

Both Ron and Tom were aware, but knew little of Stephen's previous career with the CIA. However, they knew just enough to understand that he wasn't a pure CIA desk jockey. They also had seen the man in action on occasion in recent years, including in the case when Stephen worked to protect Pope Augustine. That being the reality, when it came to Pastor Stephen Grant, they were rarely surprised by things that would otherwise be out of the ordinary for any other clergy member.

Stephen said, "Cone of silence?"

Jennifer and Maggie rolled their eyes. Ron nodded. And Tom said, "Of course."

But Zack queried, "Cone of silence?"

Tom asked, "You don't know what the cone of silence is?"

Zack shook his head. "No."

Stephen followed up, "You know, *Get Smart*."

Zack replied, "Oh, I never saw the movie."

Tom feigned outrage. "Movie? Please, no. We're talking the classic 1960s sitcom here, with Don Adams."

Zack shrugged his shoulders.

Tom continued, "Okay, Pastor Charmichael. There are certain pop culture references you need to be aware of if you're going to survive with this group. Your mission after the holidays, especially since you apparently will have a bit of free time due to Stephen picking up your Confirmation classes, is to watch a nice selection of *Get Smart*, including episodes with the cone of silence. Do you accept this assignment?"

Zack chuckled. "Yes, Tom, I do."

Tom smiled. "Good. Now, Stephen, proceed under the secrecy of the cone of silence."

Stephen gave the rundown that Matthews had given him on "An Advent for Religious Liberty," focusing mainly on the prayer services led by different churches each night throughout Advent near the tree at Rockefeller Center.

Ron sat back in his chair. "Cardinal Capriano is the type of leader who can pull this off. He has this infectious good nature about him. He seems to get along with everyone, even the media. At the same time, he is clear as to what the church teaches. He's the right man at this critical juncture."

Tom seemed to be thinking out loud. "Right after the announcement in the morning, I'm going to contact my bishop, and make sure that we're in on this." Tom's parish, St. Bart's, left the U.S. Episcopal Church due its journey away from traditional Christianity, and eventually joined the Anglican Church in North America.

Stephen responded, "Good. We're certainly onboard. It's also going to be interesting to see if any lefty churches get involved, given that Pritchett's been unfriendly to religion, especially Christianity, across the board, no differentiating between liberal or conservative, when it comes to pushing them out of the public arena."

Zack commented, "Hey, in this case, the more, the better."

Ron added, "Absolutely."

The relative quiet of their discussion was broken by Stephen bolting upright on the couch, disturbing Jennifer's head that had been resting on his shoulder. "Go, yes, go!"

Everyone in the room turned to look at the television screen that had captured Stephen's attention. The Bengals kick returner found a hole, faked around two members of the Seahawks special teams, and now was sprinting by Seattle's helpless kicker to return the second half kickoff 104 yards for a touchdown.

Stephen declared, "Ha! Maybe, you won't have that extra time on your hands, Zack, to get caught up on Agent 13."

Zack calmly advised, "Don't get too excited, Stephen. You're still behind."

Zack's calm was rewarded, as that was the last time the Bengals would score, while the Seahawks added another 17 points.

Chapter 15

All types of media attended the Monday morning press conference on the steps of St. Patrick's Cathedral, with some spilling onto Fifth Avenue itself. New York City police worked to make sure no one got hurt.

As Cardinal Capriano announced and explained "An Advent for Religious Liberty," he was met with supportive cheers from the faithful assembled with him on the steps of the gothic structure, and with shouts of disapproval from a handful of protestors positioned across Fifth Avenue.

Several Christian leaders from the city area, including Dr. Brett Matthews, made brief comments in support of "An Advent for Religious Liberty," and against religious intolerance from various groups and some in government.

It was City Councilman and Pastor Marvin Sanders who decided on the most direct response to Mayor-elect Pritchett. With his right hand in the air, pointing skyward, Sanders declared, "I am still praying to the Lord above for Adam Pritchett. It's hard to think of anyone who needs prayers more than him at this moment in this city and in this country. His arrogance apparently knows no bounds. First, he announces that he plans to work to silence churches when it comes to the life of our beloved city, and then he says that the Catholic Church, an institution that has done so much good for so many in New York, is a hate group. Let me tell you something, brothers and sisters, the only hate I see going on around here is coming from the man we just elected mayor."

Particularly with the police presence, things generally remained calm. That is, until Cardinal Capriano answered the last question from reporters. As he turned to head into the cathedral, activists hurled three tomatoes through the air towards the collection of humanity on the church steps. A cameraman, an aide to Councilman Sanders, and Cardinal Capriano were hit.

As the police moved to find the fruit hurlers, amidst commotion, complaints and some shouting, Capriano brushed the bits of tomato off his shoulder, and made a point of returning to the battery of microphones. Silence fell immediately. Capriano laughed and said, "That's okay. No harm done. Besides, I'm guessing many of our own parishioners at St. Pat's have wished they came to Mass with a few rotten tomatoes to toss my way after a homily or two."

That comment turned an ugly moment into a small victory for Cardinal Capriano.

Many of the media outlets played up the small number of protestors, presenting a story of equal forces facing off in the streets of New York City over religion, hate, faith and tolerance.

Of course, even many of the so-called "news" stories indicated that the Catholic Church and other traditional Christians interviewed by reporters were intolerant and behind the times, while the protestors – mainly militant atheists and assorted left-wing activists – were presented as being driven to the point of throwing tomatoes.

But even the most slanted piece included Cardinal Capriano's gracious and amusing comment.

Chapter 16

While Eli Cranston's body lay rotting away under dirt and leaves, Lee Morrison seemed to grow more determined by day.

He drove his 14 remaining followers ever harder, training them in firearms and hand-to-hand combat, as he tried to formulate exactly how they would go about killing Adam Pritchett. Assorted late nights at his desk had not resulted in any kind of enlightenment.

One of his followers, with a hint of doubt, had the nerve to ask, "How exactly, are we going to pull this off, Reverend?"

Morrison simply smiled, and reassuringly declared, "The Lord will make his ways clear to me. I have no doubt about that."

At lunch, he explained to the others, "The Lord has provided the first step for executing our plan. As you know, I have little tolerance for the hierarchy and bureaucracy of bodies like the Catholic Church. But the Lord has used the Catholics to provide the avenue by which we will be able to enter and work in the city without drawing any attention. This morning a cardinal announced something called 'An Advent for Religious Liberty,' whereby a bunch of churches will be praying in the city throughout Advent."

Nodding heads and an "Amen" or two was the response.

"God uses everything and everyone to fulfill His plan. And that's what He is doing with this right now. Keep in mind, I am – in fact, we are – His tools. Tools to stop evildoers like Adam Pritchett. While God will make it happen, brothers and sisters, we must be at the ready. We must be sharpened, ready tools as we act to implement His plan."

Again, nods and "Amen" rose in response.

"So, if any of you have even the tiniest of doubts, I must know now. Look deep inside. God does not have any room for doubt."

Silence lingered for a full minute.

Morrison said, "Excellent, brothers and sisters. You know, when I was watching on television this morning what these Catholics and others were planning for Advent, I had to laugh and shake my head. While prayer, obviously, is a good thing, action in the name of God is far better. We will be taking the action that these other so-called followers of God are too afraid to do. It occurred to me that this mission – to take down Adam Pritchett, tool of the devil – will be the greatest Christmas gift we could give this infected world. Am I right?"

Shouts of "Amen," and "You are so right" came back.

Morrison continued, "Yes! Amen!" He took a breath. "Now, please follow me to my office, as I have revolvers and tactical knives to give out to each of you. We will start practicing formations with those this afternoon."

Chapter 17

Carter Dujas took a sip of hot tea, and then placed the large mug down next to a laptop resting on his dining room table.

It was 9:30 PM, time for his three-way video call. A few keystrokes, and a minute later, he was looking at Perry Harris and Rollin Dawes.

The three men, who had attended college together some 15 years earlier, didn't waste time before getting down to business.

Dujas said, "Rollin, I saw your comments supporting Mayor-elect Pritchett in a few news stories. Thanks."

"I meant every word. Pritchett and ACW showed real courage in putting the right label on the Catholic Church."

Harris commented, "Like you said, meant every word."

"But now," Dawes continued, "it's time to back up words with action. We need to strike fear in these bastards, with their so-called 'Advent for Religious Liberty.' We need to make clear that they must stop bringing their religious crap – their oppression, certainly not liberty – into the public arena. They have to pay a dear price. We will make them pay that price."

Dawes' intensity radiated through dark brown eyes, slightly flared nostrils, sunken cheeks, a crew cut that had not changed since his days in the military, and gritted teeth. This contrasted with a political, almost nonchalance exhibited consistently by Dujas, and an awkward nervousness thrown off by Harris, who sported thick, dark hair and small, round glasses. Harris was far more comfortable dealing with like-minded people at the local college he taught at in Massachusetts, than the military fervor of Dawes.

"This can in no way come back on me or Pritchett," said Dujas.

Harris added, "Or on us at ACW."

Dawes seemed a bit irritated. "It's not going to come back on any of us. It's going to be carried out meticulously, under my command. New York City is now the battleground, thanks to Mayor-elect Pritchett, and we will win that battle. And I love the fact that it will be won as their Christmas approaches. I'll let you two know the time and place. You need not worry about anything."

Chapter 18

Thanksgiving Day had the potential to degrade into bedlam.

After all, in addition to Tom, Maggie, and their six children – three daughters and three sons – ranging from early teens to mid-twenties, the guests included a fiancée to the second oldest Stone daughter, two less serious dates brought by two Stone sons, Stephen and Jennifer Grant, Ron McDermott, Zack Charmichael, Joan and George Kraus with their two teenage daughters, and Michael Vanacore and his new girl friend, Melissa Ambler. Add in Maggie's mother, Nancy Chandler, and it came to twenty-two in attendance.

Thanksgiving at the Stone home – a large stone-exterior rectory sitting next to the castle-like St. Bartholomew's Anglican Church – was a first for Stephen and Jennifer. Since arriving at St. Mary's Lutheran Church years ago, Stephen had spent most Thanksgivings with his friends Hans and Flo Gunderson, until they were murdered not long after they had led the way building a new St. Mary's church building.

On the large porch of the rectory, one of the Stone offspring, the youngest son, Paul, greeted each guest upon arrival with a sheet of paper. The ever-punctual Stephen was pleased. "Check this out, Jen. It's a schedule for the day. Nice."

Jennifer looked at her husband, smiled, and said, "Excited about a schedule. Sometimes, you're so weird."

Stephen replied, "Hey, this is impressive."

Tom greeted his two friends. He looked at Jennifer, and said, "I missed it. Why is your husband weird?"

"Oh, it's just odd that he's getting excited about your schedule."

Tom corrected, "Not my schedule. That's my wife's. And I agree, it's a bit anal-retentive. But as you'll see, it actually works."

Stephen gave Jennifer and Tom a mock look of disapproval and said, "Well, at least, I will compliment Maggie on the schedule." He read it over. "So, the Stone Bowl kicks off in about an hour. Dinner at 4:30. And topped off with a movie at 7:30. What are we watching?"

Tom said, "It's a longtime tradition in the Stone household to watch *Christmas in Connecticut* on Thanksgiving."

Jennifer shook her head. "Are you serious?"

Tom looked somewhat bewildered at Jennifer and Stephen, who flashed a broad smile. "Yes, what's the deal? Problem with the movie?"

Stephen answered, "Quite the contrary. That's a wonderful film with Barbara Stanwyck."

Jennifer explained, "Stephen watches that movie every year. Has for ... how long?"

Stephen thought. "Actually, since I was a kid. In recent years, at least when the schedule permitted."

Jennifer added, "He was worried that we might not get home early enough tonight to watch his usual Thanksgiving movie, which is *White Christmas*. That kicks off about a month and a half of Christmas films for the movie buff I married."

"I also happen to be a big fan of Bing Crosby, as you both know. But Stanwyck in *Christmas in Connecticut* works nicely, too."

It was Tom's turn to shake his head. "Your wife is right. You are weird. But I've known that for a while now."

Stephen retorted, "Right, this from a guy who wears shorts and a Hawaiian shirt no matter what time of year it is as long as the temp is over 50. It's supposed to be an unseasonable 60 today, so why not the typical Tom Stone attire?"

Stephen and Jennifer were in touch football attire, as instructed by their hosts. They wore sneakers, blue jeans and a polo shirt – Stephen's a bright red with long sleeves, and Jennifer in Stephen's favorite for her, a short-sleeve pink.

Tom said, "Not today. As I told you, this is the annual Stone Bowl." Tom had sweatpants and sneakers on, but he seemed particularly proud of the blue jersey he wore, with "Stone Bowl" written across the front above a big number 1, and "Number One Dad" across the back above another big 1.

Behind Jennifer and Stephen came the Kraus family. None looked dressed for football. Joan wore brown boots, a tweed skirt and a cream-colored, lightweight, short-sleeve sweater. In his typical conservative, lawyer fashion, George was in a white, pinstriped, button-down shirt, gray pants, and black, wingtip shoes. Their daughters, Grace and Faith, who shared their mother's bright red hair, fair skin and large eyes, didn't look ready for tossing around the pigskin either in tight-fitting leggings and glittery flats.

After hugs and pecks on cheeks were exchanged, Grace and Faith hurried off to find Tom's daughters.

Stephen said, "George, you do not look dressed for touch football."

"I'm not. Bad back does not allow for football." He looked at Tom. "Not even for the Stone Bowl, Tom, sorry."

"No worries, you'll just have to eat and drink with the fans."

George replied, "I'm well equipped to do that."

Stephen turned to Joan, "And no Stone Bowl for you either, Joan?"

"Unlike Jen, I do not do football, even when it's touch."

Joan Kraus and Jennifer Grant were beyond close friends, being more like sisters. That being the case, Stephen and George claimed to be quasi-brothers-in-law.

Jennifer said, "But you do do wine." She stopped and looked quizzically. "Does that sound right? Oh well, I have a crumb cake for Maggie, so let's go see what we can do to help. She always has nice wines for the kitchen help."

Joan added, "If I had more than 20 people over for Thanksgiving, I'd be well into my second bottle by now."

As Jen and Joan moved toward the kitchen, Tom, Stephen and George followed. Eventually, Tom and Stephen moved out the backdoor and went down a few steps onto a patio. The yard behind the rectory and church was expansive, sloping gently down to a small lake.

With beers in hand, they headed in the direction of a group talking and casually tossing around a football.

This was another rare social occasion when Ron McDermott could be found in non-clerical attire, sporting tan work boots, brown pants and a long-sleeve, tan, cotton button down. Other than for golf, Stephen knew that this was about as casual as Ron got outside the St. Luke's rectory – and sometimes within the rectory.

The other four people, however, were in the full spirit of the Stone Bowl.

Zack had his Seahawks jersey on, and Tom's oldest daughter, Cara, also wore a "Stone Bowl" jersey. Cara, at 27 years old, was a younger version of her mother, including the strawberry-blond hair, but longer, bright blue eyes and smile. Stephen noticed that the two seemed more interested in each other than the football. *Well, that's intriguing.*

Stephen had not seen Mike Vanacore in a while, noting that the young, billionaire video game entrepreneur, and leading supporter of parochial education, was still sporting thick blond hair and Clark Kent glasses. Vanacore was from, and still lived in California, but also had a house on Long Island, He was an active member at St. Bart's. His football preferences were clear from his San Diego Chargers jersey.

But it was the fourth person in the group who drew Stephen's attention. He whispered to Tom, "Who is that with Mike? She looks familiar."

Stephen was referring to a tall, thin, beautiful woman with long, straight blond hair. She also had a Chargers jersey on, though cut to reveal her stomach and belly button, along with Capri-style jeans and white sneakers.

Tom answered, "Familiar? Really? Does Jen know that?"

Stephen said, "Meaning what?"

Tom continued, "That's Melissa Ambler. I guess there's no other way to put it: She's a supermodel. She and Mike have been dating for a bit. I believe she was in the most recent SI swimsuit issue."

Stephen retorted, "And how would you know that? And does Maggie know?"

"Touché. She's also been in some cosmetics commercials."

"Interesting."

Tom added, "That's not all. She's got an MBA. Mike constantly mentions her business smarts."

They stopped and looked at each other.

Stephen smirked and said, "Her business smarts. That's what he talks about constantly?"

Tom replied, "Yes, and what are you possibly implying?" His fake outrage lasted mere seconds, when they laughed, clinked their bottles, and drank some beer.

Everyone greeted Stephen warmly.

The Stone Bowl was waged in good fun, but with more than just a light touch of competitiveness, between two teams of eight. The effective St. Bart's home team – featuring the Stone family, along with Mike and Melissa – won a tight contest, with an interception by Mike returned for a touchdown to make it final.

Stephen threw the pick, and immediately knew he would not live that down with his friends – and his wife – for the entire coming year, until the next Stone Bowl.

Later, with a feast featuring two turkeys spread across two large tables arranged in a T, Tom stood and everyone fell silent.

"For those who have never been at a Stone family Thanksgiving, I officially welcome you, and thank God for your being with us. We don't do anything like putting individuals on the spot saying what they're thankful for. We leave that to each of you personally with the Lord. But I do take the opportunity to reflect a bit in our dinner prayer. So, please bow your heads."

Everyone did so.

Tom continued:

> "Dear Jesus, our Lord and Savior, we have so much to be thankful for, truly. We thank you for the family and dear friends you have brought together here today, and for the many hands that brought forth the bounty of which we are about to partake, from the farms and ranches, and every other point along the way, into our own kitchen.
>
> "But what we are most thankful for is your sacrifice and atonement for our sins, your love, forgiveness and gifts of salvation and eternal life, and your coming to us through Word and sacrament. And we thank you for your Church. While it is broken and fragmented in so many

> ways due to man's sin, it remains Your Church, and the place where believers can gather together to hear the Word, partake in the Lord's supper, learn, and help, support and strengthen each other.
>
> "Jesus, Your Church again has come under attack, with sin and the Evil One working to limit the reach of the Gospel. We pray for strength to have the courage to do what is right, to protect the Church, no matter what the price.
>
> "Finally, sweet Jesus, we pray for those who gather on this Thanksgiving, but know not who they should be thanking for their families, their friends, their blessing and their very lives. We pray that through Your grace, through the Holy Spirit, through an awakening of faith, they will come to know You.
>
> "And we pray all of this, in Your precious name. Amen."

All around the table echoed, "Amen."

Maggie looked at her husband, and squeezed his hand. She turned to her family and guests, and said, "Please, everyone, eat and enjoy."

Stephen was seated on the other side of Tom, and whispered, "Nice prayer."

Tom replied, "Thanks. All credit, of course, goes to Him." After a short pause, as he spooned some au gratin potatoes onto his plate, he added, "Although, I pondered adding thanks for that pick you threw giving us the Stone Bowl. But I thought it might make the prayer go too long."

Stephen smiled. "And so it starts. I'm never going to hear the end of this, am I?"

Tom replied, "Of course not. What are friends for?"

Chapter 19

This was the first Thanksgiving that Maureen Donahue did not spend with her family just north of Minneapolis-St. Paul in Minnesota.

She went to college in New York City, and remained there after graduating. But she always made it home for both Thanksgiving and Christmas, telling her brother and parents, "You guys know that I love New York, but not being home for the holidays would just be depressing."

Now, she sat in the darkness of her apartment in Brooklyn Heights, eating reheated, day-old Chinese food, and in the midst of a multi-day, DVD marathon catching up on the television series *Lost*, which she never saw when it was on ABC.

Her smart phone rang. She looked at the screen, and the picture of her mother and father, both smiling. They already had called her twice earlier, worried about "their little girl, alone in the big city on Thanksgiving," after just quitting her job.

When she called them right after resigning, they helped tremendously by affirming her decision without any reservations. In fact, they said that after everything they heard Pritchett saying against religion, including their own Catholic faith, they were relieved and elated that she showed, as her father put it, "the courage of her convictions, and walked away from that nutcase."

Colleagues and friends in the Democratic Party tried to assure her that walking away from Pritchett would not be held against her. All of them seem bewildered by the man they supported in his campaign to become mayor. At the same time, though, several spoke sympathetically toward what Pritchett was basically doing, just arguing that he either went too far or didn't keep the political fallout in mind.

She paused *Lost* and answered the call. It was her mother.

"Are you sure you're okay, baby?"

"Yes, Mom, I'm fine."

"You don't sound it."

"Mom, I know you're worried. Don't be. I just have to sort some things out."

"Can I help? I've always said that you can tell me anything."

Maureen paused. "Well, I'm trying to figure out if I've wasted my career."

"What do you mean? From all I can tell, you're very good at what you do, and you apparently have the respect of the people you work with, right?"

"Yes, I do. At least, I think so. But my problem is that I don't know how much I respect them anymore. These people that I've worked with for eight years now, they're kind of mystified by Pritchett."

"That's good."

"It is, as far as it goes. Several I've spoken with – too many of them, in fact – over the last few days seem to disagree with Pritchett over strategy, rather than the substance of what he was saying."

"You mean they agree with calling the Catholic Church a hate group?"

"I hate to say it, Mom, but yes, I think many of them do."

"Really?"

"I know it's hard to think so. But you have to understand, I got involved with the Democrats here in New York because they supported the same ideas and programs I did, that you and Dad do, when it comes to helping the poor and the homeless. But it's been very difficult when it comes to many other issues that you and Dad, and Father John at St. Ansgar's, for example, taught me were very important, including that God values all human life, from the very beginning to its natural end, and that from the beginning in Genesis, God made marriage for a man and a woman."

"I know, baby."

"No, Mom, it's been very hard. I've talked with some other Catholics I work with in the party, and they either disagree with the church on such things, or they merely say that there's nothing that can be done, so they concentrate on the programs for the needy. They try to compartmentalize, or place a higher priority on certain programs over things like abortion and marriage. Some claim that they agree with the church's teachings, but don't want to impose their views on others."

"Yes, we couldn't do it any longer."

"What does that mean – you couldn't do it any longer?"

"Maureen, your father and I wrestled with the same things you are now. We taught you and your brother that it was important to help the underprivileged, and that the Democrats were the party that did that. But things have changed dramatically in recent times, and not for the better. We couldn't ignore the opposition to so much of our faith, and it became increasingly clear that many of those programs we supported don't seem to work very well either."

"Mom, what are you saying?"

"We didn't want to tell you, given your work, but a few years ago, your father and I became, well, Republicans."

Maureen stood up, knocking over her sesame chicken. "Oh, my God. My social justice, liberal Catholic parents have become Republicans?"

"Yes. I guess you'd even call us kind of conservatives now. We watch a lot of Fox News, too."

"What?!"

"There's more. Your brother has joined the Young Republicans at school."

"What? Mark is a YR! How did all of this happen?"

"Maureen, baby, we just came to the conclusion that, if we prioritize issues according to our faith, we couldn't remain Democrats."

"I don't know about that, Mom."

"Maureen, think about the troubling reactions you've heard firsthand on this entire anti-religion, anti-Catholic crusade launched by the man who was just elected mayor of New York City – your own boss."

Maureen and her mother fell silent.

"Maureen, are you still there?"

"Yes, I'm here."

"I'm sorry, baby. I didn't mean to hurt you. I know how passionate you are about your career and about politics. Did I hurt you?'

"No, Mom. Of course not. But you sure have added to the things that I have to think about."

"This is the personal journey that your father and I have gone on. Mark embarked on his own journey as well, and you have to come to your own conclusions. In the end, Maureen, just know that I love you."

"I know, Mom. I love you, too. Can we talk again tomorrow? I want to get some rest."

"Sure, baby."

They said their quick good-byes, and hung up.

Maureen sat staring at the frozen scene on the television screen for another ten minutes. She finally cleaned up the sesame chicken, clicked the "Play" button on the remote, laid down on the couch, pulled a blanket up, and proceeded to watch the rest of season four of *Lost*.

Chapter 20

Mayor Hal Richardson was on his way out after two terms as mayor of New York. Richardson was plagued throughout his second term by accusations of not being tough enough on crime.

During this recent campaign, while on the sidelines, he was annoyed by the fact that a fellow Democrat, running to be his successor, effectively threw him under the political bus on the crime issue.

Richardson had no love for Adam Pritchett.

Now, with all of the controversy stirred up by Pritchett's militant atheism on display, Richardson was being treated better by the media and assorted interest groups than he had been over the past three years. During this lame duck session, Richardson suddenly became more relevant than he'd been in some time, and it was apparent to most that he was enjoying the attacks on his successor. He told a reporter, "Suddenly, I don't look so bad, do I?"

Across his large, ornate desk in City Hall sat three clergy members who had been very active working with city government on a variety of poverty and housing initiatives.

They were anxious and nervous, and pleading with the outgoing mayor.

Anne Abrams, a pastor in the Evangelical Lutheran Church in America, or ELCA, dressed in dark gray slacks and blazer, a light gray shirt with clerical collar, asked, "What are we supposed to do, Mr. Mayor?"

Seated to Abram's right was Barney Flanders, in his black Episcopal bishop attire, along with long, swept-back gray hair. He was twirling and swinging a large gold cross on a chain around his neck. "Is Mayor-elect Pritchett serious when talking about cutting off all city funding, even to our churches? If he wants to bash the Catholic Church, so be it. But why us? We're all open-minded, Progressive."

To the left of Abrams was Pastor Norman Scott, a black Methodist minister from Harlem. With his dark, thick hair, beard and mustache, combined with being six-foot-four and weighing in at more than 300 pounds, Scott was never lost in the crowd. "Does Pritchett have any clue as to what our churches mean to the poor communities in this city?"

Richardson smiled. It appeared to be an attempt to soothe, but a smile never quite fit right on Hal Richardson. His face was dominated by a large, bulging forehead and black bushy eyebrows. Everything else receded from there – thinning hair, narrow eyes, small ears and nose, thin mouth with only a trace of lips, and practically no chin.

Despite the smile, Richardson's answers amounted to little more than "I don't know" to each person. But he added, "Trust me, I know how valuable your work is to New York, and I pledge to make that clear to my successor. Mayor-elect Pritchett obviously has a lot to learn. To a certain degree, that has to be expected from people who have never held elected office before. But this unprecedented hostility to faith communities, particularly the ones that you represent, goes beyond anything we've heard before. It's particularly distressing that he's a Democrat. I will speak with him, and try to reason with him. You have my word."

After the three ministers left, Mayor Richardson told his assistant to get in contact with Pritchett's office, and that they needed to speak some time that day.

Later that Friday afternoon, Richardson's assistant finally received word from Adam Pritchett's office. She timidly approached Richardson's desk. "Mr. Mayor?"

"Yes, Susan. Did Pritchett finally get back?"

"Well, sir, I'm sorry, but Mr. Pritchett's assistant just got back to me."

"And?"

"Um..."

"Out with it, Susan."

"His assistant said that Mayor-elect Pritchett was dealing with a variety of issues, and would not have time to speak with you any time soon. But she did say that the Mayor-elect had time in a week."

Richardson yelled, "What?"

"Um, next Friday."

"Next Friday!" Richardson was shouting.

"I know, sir. I reminded her that this was a request from you, Mayor Richardson. But she cut me off, and suggested I get back to her shortly."

"I don't believe that arrogant son of a bitch."

Chapter 21

In little more than a day, the weather changed dramatically. Saturday was rainy and raw.

Maureen Donahue had not ventured from her apartment, other than two quick runs to a local grocery store, in more than five days.

She had finished up the sixth and last season of *Lost* early that afternoon, and then had a late lunch consisting of a peanut butter and grape jelly sandwich.

Maureen then showered, and slipped on blue jeans, a dark blue mock turtleneck, black boots, and a raincoat. With an umbrella shielding her from the blowing, cold raindrops, she made her way to the Number 2 Subway, riding the train into Manhattan and getting off at the Time Square stop. Despite the worsening rain, she walked over from Seventh Avenue and Broadway to Fifth Avenue, turning north for eight blocks.

She entered St. Patrick's Cathedral a few minutes after 5:00 PM.

Since moving to New York City, Maureen had limited attendance at Mass, perhaps three or four times a year, other than when she went home for holidays.

While tourists moved about at the fringes of the sanctuary, Mass proceeded.

Maureen was visibly distracted by the noise.

But it was clear that the Old Testament reading from Malachi 3:13-18 caught her attention.

The priest read: "'Your words have been hard against me, says the Lord. But you say, "How have we spoken against you?" You have said, "It is vain to serve God. What is the profit of keeping his charge or walking as in mourning before the Lord of hosts? And now we call the arrogant blessed. Evildoers not only prosper but they put God to the test and they escape."'"

A tear formed in the corner of one eye.

The priest read on: "Then those who feared the Lord spoke with one another. The Lord paid attention and heard them, and a book of remembrance was written before him of those who feared the Lord and esteemed his name. 'They shall be mine, says the Lord of hosts, in the day when I make up my treasured possession, and I will spare them as a man spares his son who serves him. Then once more you shall see the distinction between the righteous and the wicked, between one who serves God and one who does not serve him.'"

Tears gently moved down her round cheeks. She looked at the pew rack in front of her, found and opened a Bible. Maureen looked quickly in the page of contents for Malachi. She flipped pages. Her finger arrived at the following verse unread by the priest.

"'For behold, the day is coming, burning like an oven, when all the arrogant and all evildoers will be stubble. The day that is coming shall set them ablaze, says the Lord of hosts, so that it will leave them neither root nor branch.'"

More tears fell.

Chapter 22

Cardinal Capriano, Dr. Brett Matthews, Episcopal Bishop Barney Flanders, and several other New York City metro area clergy sat around the large conference room table in the St. Patrick's Cathedral Parish House.

An additional 72 clergy members and church leaders from across the country had dialed in for the meeting.

They opened with prayer, a reminder of what was at stake, with a leading traditional Catholic and a far more liberal Catholic speaking to the issue, followed by Dr. Matthews and Bishop Flanders also bringing different perspectives – but with all coming to the same conclusion. That is, this attack on religious liberty cannot stand unanswered.

An aide to Cardinal Capriano then gave a rundown on the schedule for how this "Advent for Religious Liberty" would work, in particular reviewing which church would be taking the lead for the prayer vigils each evening near the Rockefeller Center tree. The aide apologized, again, to the churches that could not be fit into the three-plus weeks to lead one of the prayer gatherings.

The aide added, "So, that's the prayer vigil schedule throughout Advent here in New York City. As was mentioned earlier, we have spoken with Mayor Richardson about security and where it makes sense for us to be. Given the tremendous response, which I relayed to him, the police will be blocking off 48th Street, between Fifth and the Avenue of the Americas each night during Advent from eight to ten. If the prayer vigils get under way each night around 8:30 and finish up an hour later, that'll work nicely in terms of logistics of getting people there and out."

After many questions from those in the room and over the telephone lines were answered, reports about similar efforts across the nation were heard.

Cardinal Capriano said, "I want to thank each of you and your respective churches for coming together like this, despite our various differences, as one, united Christian family to stand up for religious liberty. It's been a true blessing to see the response here in New York, and to hear about the plans in other parts of the country. By the way, Mayor Richardson did not have to block off 48th Street, so if you get a chance, please send along a thank you to his office. Are there any other questions?"

Three callers buzzed in with statements, rather than questions. But the faces around the table seemed to show appreciation, for they echoed the need for all Christians to come together in this time of, as one caller put it, "persecution of the Church right here in the United States."

Cardinal Capriano then moved to wrap things up. "Please, let us pray for each other throughout this time of attack on our faith, on the Church. Let's close out today's meeting with the Lord's Prayer."

On the way out of the building, Dr. Matthews wound up walking next to Bishop Flanders.

Matthews said, "Well, Barney, at least it's good to see you at something beyond the occasional bumping into each other at a charity event."

"Yes, unfortunate, though."

Matthews raised an eyebrow, and said, "Excuse me?"

Flanders laughed. "No, I didn't mean it that way. I mean that it's unfortunate it takes an attack like this for us to see each other and work together."

Matthews returned the smile. "On that, we are in agreement."

They exchanged handshakes and wishes for God's blessings on the sidewalk of 51st Street, and went their separate ways.

Chapter 23

After much yelling and cursing the week before, Mayor Richardson actually agreed to talk with his successor on this Friday morning. However, Richardson had gotten even more frustrated by the insistence that he come to the Pritchett Building. None of this was something that was done to a mayor of New York City. But eventually, again, he agreed.

As Richardson was shown into the spacious, 19th floor office, Pritchett looked up from and then back to one of the computer screens on his U-shaped desk. A couple of keystrokes, and then he rose, walked across the room, and extended a handshake.

"Hal, it's wonderful to see you."

"Adam, how are you?"

"Very well. Please sit down."

Pritchett returned to his black leather seat at the desk that dominated the room.

Richardson looked at the small, armless, straight-back chair that was offered as his place. "No, thank you, Adam." He walked to the large windows and looked out. "I'll stand."

"Suit yourself. Now, what did we need to discuss?"

Richardson said, "Adam, I'm not going to waste your time. You've made quite clear how valuable you judge that time to be, especially compared to the time of others."

"Yes, it is."

Richardson continued, "So, do you mind if I provide a little advice from someone who has been around the political block several times?"

Pritchett failed to hide his exasperation with a deep sigh. "Of course, Hal, I'm always interested in how I can further the successes and fix the failures of my predecessors."

Richardson clenched his fists, and bit what little lower lip he had. He walked over to the desk, and looked down on Pritchett. "You're going to pay dearly for calling the Catholic Church a hate group, and your idea for trying to push religious groups out of the city's public life not only is dumb, but will turn out to be a tremendous drain on you and your administration."

Pritchett leaned back, and with his elbows resting on the arms of his chair, he made a triangle with his hands and rested his chin on the tip. "I obviously disagree, Hal."

The two men stared at each other in silence.

Richardson shook his head, and strolled back to the floor-to-ceiling windows. "Several leaders from religious institutions that work with the city have come to me in recent days to see if I could bang some common sense into your head."

Pritchett laughed. "Common sense from religious groups. That's contradictory."

"You are clueless. We're obviously done. My people will, of course, work to make for a seamless transition to your administration."

Pritchett had returned to a computer screen. "Thank you, Hal, that's appreciated."

Richardson walked to the office door. Before opening it, he looked back at Pritchett. "Adam, you're a fool, and unless you stop being a fool, you'll go down as one of the worst mayors in this city's history."

Pritchett replied, "That's rich coming from you, Hal."

"Kiss my ass, Pritchett." Mayor Richardson slammed the door on his way out.

Chapter 24

It was the first Sunday of Advent, and the first gathering in "An Advent for Religious Liberty."

The Archdiocese of New York was scheduled to lead the first prayer vigil that night. The Rockefeller Center tree was still being set up, to be lit in three days.

Some 15 minutes after 48th Street was closed off between Fifth and Sixth Avenues, the entire area was flooded with people. On the stage for the gathering, with music emanating from speakers, a small choir from a Catholic church in Queens sang "Come, Thou Long Expected Jesus" and then "O Come, O Come, Emmanuel."

Many in the crowd joined in, with the words on three large video screens. Stephen and Jennifer Grant were among those singing.

When the hymn ended, Cardinal Capriano welcomed everyone in his warm, robust way. He went on to lead a modified Vespers prayer service. After several thousand people finished singing "The Advent of Our King," Capriano gave his homily, focusing on the Gospel reading that day from Luke 21, with Jesus speaking about how He will return, and that it will be a time of tumult, confusion and fear. Capriano then noted, "Of course, Jesus tells us how we can stand strong against these many and dire storms. He says, 'But stay awake at all times, praying that you may have strength to escape all these things that are going to take place, and to stand before the Son of Man.'"

Capriano continued, "There are times when Jesus says that we would have to pray and stand strong against persecution of His Church. We are in the midst of such persecution right now, that is, the efforts to exclude the Church from speaking out in public on moral issues, to stop us from participating in public acts of compassion and charity, and slandering the Catholic Church as a hate group. That is not what the United States of America is about. We are a nation born, in part, of religious liberty, not a nation whereby government, at whatever level, seeks to suppress such liberty."

While listening to Cardinal Capriano, Stephen experienced an old feeling, a warning. From his earliest days with the CIA, on rare occasions, he would get a tightening in his head and ears, like pressure building. That experience always preceded something dangerous occurring. He called these "red alerts."

Stephen pulled Jennifer closer.

She looked at him. "What is it?"

He scanned the crowd, but could only see so far. None of those around him made suspicious movements.

Just beyond Grant's line of sight, though, was Rollin Dawes. He moved slowly, but never ceased circulating. He barely hid his disgust when glancing at the Cardinal speaking at the microphone.

Beyond Dawes were two men in their mid-twenties. They didn't try to hide the beer cans in brown paper bags. They paid no attention to what Capriano said. Nor did the people around them seem of interest. Instead, they were drawn to the many media members and cameras. They pointed at the cameras atop news vans, talked and laughed. The two men looked alike, dark, buzz cut hair, oversized teeth and lips that rarely closed, narrow eyes, thick eyebrows and muscular bodies. Both dressed in jeans, a hoodie and baseball cap. The similarities were unsurprising to those who knew that they were brothers – Chad and Tray Payne. But even back home in Vermont, few people really knew Chad and Tray, who were not around much, and when they were, wound up in skirmishes after drinking far too much.

On the stage, Capriano concluded, "And by the way, as I look at the thousands gathered here tonight, fellow Catholics, our other brothers and sisters in Christ, and the rest of God's children, I do not see hate. All I see is God's love."

Meanwhile, Grant looked around. *A false red alert?* Still, even as each minute passed and nothing happened, and his red alert eased, he was not comfortable. *Maybe a red alert warning?*

Chapter 25

While extremely rare for your typical Lutheran pastor, talking one-on-one with a Catholic prelate didn't rank as all that unusual for Pastor Stephen Grant.

Now, he was on the phone with Cardinal Capriano. "So, Pastor Grant, Dr. Matthews has given me a flavor of your previous career. I've also been briefed on your work regarding Pope Augustine. As a result, here we are. I understand that you have some concerns about security for the Advent prayer services?"

Okay, can't explain my red alerts to this man.

"Well, Cardinal Capriano, perhaps it's better to say that I always have concerns about events such as this that are charged with controversy, whether or not such controversy is legitimate."

"Yes?"

"Don't get me wrong. The NYPD, from what I've seen and what I know of their skills, probably has most key aspects of security covered."

"From what I have been briefed on, that most certainly is the case."

"But I'm also of the school of thought that, in situations like this, bringing additional eyes and experience to the table can be a big plus."

"Meaning?"

"In my former career with the CIA, I worked with some of the best people at identifying and dealing with security risks of all kinds."

Capriano chuckled. "You want me to contact the CIA?"

"No, sir, I do not. This would not be within the CIA's purview. However, I would like to suggest a team that is no longer with the CIA, but instead is a private security firm."

Capriano sighed. "Do you really think this is necessary, Pastor Grant?"

Grant did not hesitate. "Yes, I absolutely do."

The Cardinal was silent for a few seconds. Grant assumed he was weighing his options.

Capriano said, "Well, Pastor Grant, several people have told me that you should be listened to on matters such as this. I'll have to think about it. But please give me the information on this team, and how we can get in contact with them."

Grant provided Capriano with all of the necessary information to get in contact with his former CIA partner, Paige Caldwell.

Before they hung up, Grant added, "Two things before I let you go, Cardinal Capriano."

"Yes."

"First, thank you for taking action against this attack on Christianity."

"Thank you, Pastor Grant. But we would be negligent if we did not act."

"And second, if you decide to contact Ms. Caldwell, I advise not allowing that information to go beyond your inner circle until you speak with her."

Chapter 26

The big Christmas tree was lit at 8:00 PM, with the crowd erupting.

Next up in terms of the musical acts to perform for those standing in the nippy air swirling around Rockefeller Center, and the millions seated comfortably and watching on television in their warm homes, was Call Us Men, a nineties "boy band" in the midst of a wildly successful comeback tour that featured a new album.

One block south, a few thousand Christians were gathering for that evening's prayers in "An Advent for Religious Liberty." The large video screens announced that the service would begin after the tree festivities were finished at nine.

While waiting, some simply listened to the performers under the tree, while others gathered in small circles to pray and read from Holy Scripture.

That peaceful scene would later be contrasted by the media with what was about to come just a block or so west.

The Payne brothers had wedged their old, rusting, white van between two tourist buses on 48th Street just off Seventh Avenue. The vehicle sat there for 20 minutes, until a police officer took notice. Seeing no one in the driver or passenger seat, he banged on the side. "Hey, anybody inside?" He looked around for an approaching driver.

The back doors of the van swung open. The officer walked to the back. "Hey, you gotta get this thing outta here. And it's ticket time..."

He stopped talking when seeing two individuals dressed from head to toe in black. Both were helmeted, masked and covered in thick body armor. They carried AK-47 assault rifles, with two additional rifles hanging on the backs of each man. Their armored suits also carried handguns and additional ammunition.

The officer reached for his weapon. But he never made it. A spray of armor piercing rounds dropped him to the street.

Screams and shouts followed from all around, with people scrambling to move away from the scene.

The Payne brothers walked east, toward Sixth Avenue. They stopped at the windows of Fox News, and sprayed the large, ground level windows with a hail of bullets.

A wave of humanity moved away from the two assailants. That wave indiscriminately crashed into other people, vehicles and buildings. Two security guards moved against the wave. One managed to get two shots off that actually hit Chad Payne in the chest. But the rounds bounced off harmlessly.

A spray of bullets from Tray's AK-47 took down each guard.

A few yards away, a police officer radioed the emergency to all. "We need ESU and serious firepower. We've got assholes shooting things up. They're armored and seem to be carrying a freakin' armory. It's North Hollywood all over. Move it." He added, "Looks like they're heading towards Sixth and the people on 48th."

Charlie Driessen heard the police chatter, and relayed the information to his partners, Paige Caldwell and Sean McEnany.

All three had ties to Pastor Stephen Grant. Paige Caldwell and Charlie Driessen had worked with Stephen

Grant at the CIA years ago, and the ever-mysterious McEnany was a member of St. Mary's parish. Caldwell, however, had been Grant's partner in and out of bed those years past. The three now worked together as an independent contractor for the CIA and others. Although, McEnany was part-time, with his fulltime job as vice president with a firm that did security for both private firms and for the government.

McEnany said, "Shit, already, we just got here. I'm not even set up."

McEnany and Driessen were getting organized in a third floor office on the east end of 48th Street between Fifth and Sixth Avenues, with big windows looking down on the prayer service area, while Paige was doing the same thing in a fourth floor corner office at the other end of that section of 48th.

Stephen happened to be meeting with Paige, bringing her up to speed on the entire "Advent for Religious Liberty" background and events.

Paige moved to a window looking out on Sixth. "Charlie, I see them. These two are fully protected. It's either heavy enough rounds to get through that armor, some kind of explosive, or face shots."

Grant looked as well. "Dear God." *Lord, please help us.* "Paige, you can make the shot."

Paige was already grabbing a Swiss SSG550 sniper rifle. She had gained an appreciation for this weapon from Grant years ago.

The first thing Paige had done when arriving earlier was to unseal the windows in case of emergency.

"No, Stephen, you're the sniper. You can make this shot."

"I've been away too long," Stephen said, shaking his head. He picked up a Glock 20 from a gun suitcase, along with a tactical knife. "You take it. I'm going down there to see what I can do."

Caldwell ignored Grant as she quickly and efficiently finished setting up the rifle. She muttered, "And of course, at night with lights moving all around."

Grant effectively slid down the three sets of stairs. When he finally got out onto Sixth Avenue, he was amazed that some traffic was still moving on the road, even as shots rang out, and panicked mobs fled on foot.

The police had slowed down the Payne brothers. But once the three officers were shot, the two killers resumed their movement to cross the avenue.

Grant decided his only chance was to circle around. The Payne brothers did not seem all that concerned with what was behind them.

Grant sprinted across the avenue. In the corner of his eye, he noticed a few of the fleeing crowd stopping to look at him. *What the hell...?* Then he recalled that he was wearing clergy attire. Even amidst the horror of two armored men shooting their way across midtown Manhattan, a few people were just as shocked to see a pastor or priest running across Sixth Avenue with a gun in one hand and a rather large knife in the other.

Grant had completely circled behind the Payne brothers. He now saw that from behind, there was no shot. Their helmets came down too low and their armor up too high. *Nothing.* He realized what had to be done. *Crap.*

But he was fully back in his Navy SEAL and CIA days. There was no time for hesitation, or doubt. Lives were at stake. Grant had to close in and act.

As his first movements were taken toward the men who had now stepped out onto Sixth Avenue, Grant saw the head of the one on the right explode in splattered flesh and blood. He fell back to the ground.

Thank you, Paige.

Chad Payne looked down at his dead brother, and screamed in rage. He looked back up, scanning for the person who fired the shot.

Grant sprinted closer.

Chad screamed again, and pressed the trigger on his rifle, firing rounds into fleeing innocents and stopped vehicles.

Lord, please.

Grant dropped the gun and landed on Chad Payne's back. He pushed down on Payne's rifle, so the bullets started going into the ground rather than into people. And with his left hand, Grant swung the tactical knife around and plunged it into Chad's neck. Grant turned and pulled hard.

The effect was nearly instantaneous. No more gunfire. The rifle fell away harmlessly. Chad Payne then slipped from this world, and down onto Sixth Avenue.

Stephen Grant stood breathing heavily, with blood dripping from the knife still in his hand.

In the window above, Paige Caldwell murmured, "You can still get the job done, Stephen Grant."

The first NYPD officer to reach Grant had a look of bewilderment on his face. He kept his gun drawn. "Uh, thanks, Father? Um, you okay?"

Grant looked at the man. "Yes, I'm fine, officer."

Other members of the NYPD moved in close.

One officer said, "Never saw anything like that before. What kind of priest are you, anyway?"

Grant replied. "Actually, I'm a Lutheran pastor."

Another cop asked, "Shit, do all Lutheran pastors kick ass like that?"

Grant was still working to regain his bearings. He answered rather absentmindedly. "No, probably not."

"Well, sure glad you do." The cop shook his hand.

With the immediate threat gone, the focus of each person switched to the death and injuries in the area. Each officer moved to help, as did Grant, who also prayed silently.

Chapter 27

"Seems like you're a hit with the press again."

Jennifer Grant just came back into the house with the newspapers from the end of the driveway. She held up the *New York Post* with a headline declaring "Knife-Toting Clergy Stops Murder Spree."

This was the second time that Stephen had put a stop to a shooting spree, and the New York media did not miss this fact.

The police and the FBI had whisked Grant away from the scene the night before. But there was no mistaking his involvement, especially since it had been caught on video and shown on television and the Internet. The NYPD put out an innocuous statement about Grant's involvement, and his experience with the SEALS and CIA. There was no mention of Paige Caldwell. The sniper shot taking down one of the Payne brothers was attributed to "law enforcement personnel."

Stephen was preparing breakfast for his wife who had welcomed him home with warm, embracing love in the middle of the night.

Over western omelets, they discussed the news and fallout of the previous night's events.

While clicking along on her laptop, Jennifer noted, "Pritchett isn't giving any ground. He put out a statement apparently. He said, and I quote, 'The bravery of our law enforcement personnel was on full display in this crisis. All New Yorkers owe them a huge debt of gratitude.' But then he added, 'It's also important to keep in mind that the actions of these two madmen have nothing to do with my statements on the role of religion in public life, or any other statements of people in public life on any issues.'"

Stephen said, "Well, at least, he's right about that."

"You think?"

"As much as Pritchett's dead wrong about pretty much everything else in this entire mess, he can't be blamed for these two murderers."

"Fair enough."

They ate and read silently for a few minutes. And then Jennifer stopped and looked at her husband. "I have to ask you something."

"What is it, Jen?"

She took a deep breath. "I saw what you did on television last night."

Stephen was not sure what was coming next.

Jennifer continued, "I have to admit that there are times when I have a tough time thinking of you as a SEAL or a CIA operative, given what kind of husband and pastor you are. But then I think back on how you once saved others and me at St. Mary's. And even with the violence I saw on that video, I understand that you helped save so many people. And that makes me very proud of you."

Stephen smiled at his wife.

Jennifer added, "But my question is: How do you separate the two – the violence versus everything else that you do that is gentle and caring?"

Good question.

"That's not the easiest thing to answer. When I was a SEAL and with the CIA, it seemed simple. It was my job. It was what I did for my country. And unlike some of my brothers and sisters in that line of work, I never saw that work conflicting with my faith. I was doing the right thing.

I still think I was doing the right thing back then. As for these occasions when my old life presents situations where the old Stephen has to act, that's how I have to think of it. I'm put in a situation where my old skills and abilities have to be used to do the right thing. I don't have a problem with that, even as a pastor now. But from the day I entered the Navy, there's always a challenge to make sure the violence stays where the violence should be, and does not leak into other areas of life. Most of the people I've worked with understand that and don't struggle with it. But I've known a few who could not do it. Does that make sense?"

"Yes, I think so."

"In the end, I put it all in God's hands, asking Him for His help and grace. And the wonderful thing is that He sent me you to keep it all in perspective, and to keep me grounded in what's really important."

Jennifer got up from the table, grabbed their two empty plates, leaned down and kissed Stephen. She said, "Good answer."

Chapter 28

As he entered, FBI Supervisory Special Agent Rich Noack declared, "What are you running, Caldwell, a jobs program for former CIA?"

"Funny, Noack. I like to think of it as a private firm that bails out government bureaucrats like you."

Noack and Caldwell worked together previously, and liked each other.

Following Noack was Trent Nguyen, one of the most decorated active FBI agents. Nguyen was slim and tall at six feet two inches. But even he was dwarfed by the six-foot-six Noack.

The two FBI agents, both in blue suits and white shirts, with Noack's tie red and Nguyen's yellow, contrasted sharply with Caldwell and Charlie Driessen. Paige was striking, with long black hair, now pulled back in a ponytail, gray-blue eyes, and a firm body that fit nicely in cargo-style pants, a t-shirt and multi-pocketed jacket – all in black. Meanwhile, Driessen had lost most of his hair, sported an unruly gray mustache, and wore tan pants, a wrinkled yellow shirt and well-worn navy blue blazer.

The four shook hands, and sat down at the conference room table in the Jacob K. Javits Federal Building in downtown Manhattan.

Noack began, "Thanks for your work yesterday. Among so much death, your team saved lives."

Paige replied, "We were lucky to have arrived just a couple of hours earlier."

Noack continued, "Speaking of your 'we,' I know Grant's not an official team member, obviously, but where is Sean McEnany?"

Caldwell glanced at Driessen and smiled. "Sean works according to his own schedule. He has multiple commitments."

"So, we've heard," added Nguyen. "He's quite a mystery."

Driessen agreed, "And not just to you, guys, trust me. At the same time, he's damn good. I've seen it firsthand."

Nguyen said, "The little that we have on McEnany would agree with that."

Noack looked at Caldwell. "Listen, I've gotten clearance to hire your team for this Advent stretch. I want your expertise and abilities with us."

Caldwell replied, "I'm flattered, Rich, but we have an employer in this case – the Catholic Archdiocese of New York."

"Yes, I know. I spoke with Cardinal Capriano, and he is exceedingly pleased to have the FBI on the ground and agreed that your team should be working with us as well."

Caldwell smirked. "I don't know if I like working for the FBI. Kind of goes against my CIA roots."

Noack jibed back. "Well, it's either us or no one."

"Alright, then we're on board with you FBI boys. Understand, though, that our government rates are higher than what we charge nice nonprofits like the Catholic Church. You know, all those added headaches and paperwork that come with government work."

"Send us the invoice, and you can haggle with our accountants. More importantly, we have a rundown on these Payne brothers."

Driessen said, "Good, what was the deal with those bastards?"

Nguyen explained, "They apparently have nothing to do with the debate over whether or not the Catholic Church is a hate group, nor on this attack or challenge that Mayor-elect Pritchett is putting forth against religion in general."

"What then?" asked Driessen, with irritation in his voice.

"From what our agents put together from their home, family, former teachers, and their limited number of friends and acquaintances, they were aggravated with the media. Did not matter if it was right, left or center. At the same time, they were fascinated by news stories of the outrageous and the violent."

Caldwell jumped in, "I know this is speculative still. But are you saying that these two brothers were just looking to make news?"

Nguyen replied, "That very well could be. And notice that they shot the windows out at Fox, and it easily could be that they were heading over to the NBC studios, rather than specifically attacking the prayer vigil. In addition, we combed their Internet viewing, and much of it had to with videos of real-life shootings and murders, including the 1997 North Hollywood battle between two armored bank robbers and the police."

Driessen added, "The first cop to call in the shooting actually said that it looked like we have another North Hollywood on our hands."

"That's right," replied Nguyen. "And the two events have an eerie similarity."

"Shit, two assholes looking to get on TV," injected Driessen.

Noack cut in. "We'll obviously keep you up to date as we get more on these two. But as you know, Paige, we've got to stay on top of things going forward. Just because there's been one incident doesn't mean there cannot be others."

Paige agreed, "We've learned that the hard way too many times."

Noack said, "We like the set up you have in those two offices. In addition to other spots we have, those are nice perches. How did you land them?"

Caldwell replied, "Actually, I'm not really sure. You'd have to ask Sean."

Noack raised an eyebrow and glanced at Nguyen.

Caldwell added, "Like Charlie said, he's a mystery in many ways to us. But he gets the job done."

Noack said, "We want you to stay there, and we'll give you a full rundown on where else we and NYPD's Emergency Service Unit are positioned."

"Good."

"Also," Noack noted, "we have a contact within Pritchett's office."

Caldwell smiled. "The FBI spying on elected officials? Rich, what is this world coming to?"

"Knock if off. We're not spying on Pritchett. A member of his staff owes us big time, and we have concerns about another member. He has some associations – one in particular – that warrants watching during this religious dust up."

Chapter 29

The night after the shootings, the largest crowd yet turned out for "An Advent for Religious Liberty."

Those numbers were matched by a massive police and FBI presence, including four mobile platforms raised to three stories high with armed personnel standing atop watching and guarding the crowd. In contrast to such prominence, local and federal law enforcement also moved stealthily among the gathering in plain clothes, watching, assessing and calculating.

Entrances from buildings onto that part of 48th Street were closed off, with people entering slowly via lanes carved out of blockades at both Fifth and Sixth Avenue, and via the Rockefeller Plaza pathway from 49th Street and the tree.

At 8:30, a large choir in blue and white robes from Brooklyn's Agape A.M.E. Church raised the spirit and energy of those gathered with stirring renditions of "Swing Low, Sweet Chariot," "Amazing Grace," and "Go Down Moses."

The Reverend Marvin Sanders, also a member of the city council, stepped up to the microphone, wearing a red robe over a black suit and tie, and white shirt.

Sanders' deep voice echoed through the canyon formed by skyscrapers.

"Brothers and sisters, welcome. God's grace upon all of you.

"As I look out at this huge gathering, after the horrific shootings last night, I cannot help but see the work of the Holy Spirit.

"Let us take a moment to pray.

"Dear Lord, please welcome into your Kingdom those who lost their lives yesterday, and care for their families and friends. And Lord, we pray for healing for those who were injured both physically and emotionally. And finally, thank you, God, for those brave souls who stopped the evildoers among us from killing and hurting further. Amen."

He paused, and "Amen" rang out from the crowd.

"That last spiritual we heard and sang – 'When Israel Was in Egypt's Land' – has always had a deep meaning for the African-American community. The Israelites were in slavery to the Egyptians. And of course, our own nation had a shameful history of enslaving the black race.

"And while we were most certainly free in Jesus – that's right, even as slaves we were free in Christ – we needed and had a right to our earthly freedom.

"Blood was spilled in the Civil War for freedom. For the 150 years since, the fight has been against racism and for our full civil rights. And we think about our brother, Martin Luther King, Jr., who declared, 'I have a dream that my four little children will one day live in a nation where they will not be judged by the

> color of their skin, but by the content of their character.'
>
> "We're not there yet. But we're closer than ever before in this nation. That dream is still alive, brothers and sisters.
>
> "But now we have a man who I know, or at least I thought I knew, who is about to become mayor of our great city. This man, Adam Pritchett, wants to take away that which even the slave masters and the pharaohs were unable to do. He wants to take away our voices as Christians. Oh sure, Pritchett and his types say that you can do what you want in your churches, your synagogues and your homes, but not in the public life of the city. Well, I don't know about you, brothers and sisters, but I try to be all about my faith at home, in church, in public, and in my career. He wants to take away our voices as people of faith in our government, in the choices that are made by elected officials, and in the services that are delivered for the needy among us.
>
> "And he has the nerve to say that the Catholic Church is a hate group. Are you as outraged and angry as I am, my friends?"

A large part of those gathered answered with shouts, like "Amen!" and "Yes, brother!"

> "Good. You should be.
>
> "We must be like Moses, and shout against the power of Pharaoh Pritchett. Tell him to 'Let my people go.'
>
> "Oh, let us all from bondage flee."

Those gathered responded, "Let My people go."

"And let us all in Christ be free."

The crowd: "Let My people go."

"Go down, Moses, way down to Egypt's land,
Tell old Pharaoh."

The crowd: "Let My people go."

Sanders concluded: "Yes, indeed, it's time for Pharaoh-elect Adam Pritchett to let God's people go."

The crowd jammed into 48th Street cheered.

Trent Nguyen was one of the FBI in the crowd. He was moving with a purpose, following one person that he knew for a fact was out of place – Rollin Dawes, head of Patriotic Atheists for America.

Chapter 30

It was a little after eight on Friday morning, and Rich Noack and Trent Nguyen were back in the conference room in the Javits building with a team of a dozen agents.

Noack was laying out links uncovered between two people in Adam Pritchett's orbit, and the leader of an atheist group with a militaristic bent and, in turn, his contacts with persons of interest.

Noack had all of the faces, names and affiliations up on a screen. "To sum up, Dujas, who is Pritchett's right hand man, Harris, who leads this Atheists for a Caring World, and Dawes, leader of Patriotic Atheists for America, all went to college together. Davenport has made clear to us that Dujas is more hard-core, even radical in his atheism, than is Pritchett. Meanwhile, Dawes blames the Catholic Church for the suicide of his brother, and Agent Nguyen spotted him at the prayer service last night. Finally, we just found out that at least two times since Thanksgiving, Dawes has met with these four – Lindell, Barletta, Weiner and Jennings. Each of them is a person of interest to the FBI."

Nguyen jumped in to give a rundown on Sam Lindell, Wanda Barletta, Nate Weiner and Ned Jennings. They were known as weapons experts for hire, including explosives. But being very careful, none were yet to be arrested for the major crimes they were under suspicion for, including bringing about eight deaths between them.

After a series of questions, Noack concluded, "We should have enough to get warrants for phone taps and records, along with Internet searches, and so on. We're also going to get eyes on this entire group. Let's get on this people. Thanks."

Chapter 31

A bell rang on a Christmas tree.

Zuzu pointed to the bell, and said, "Look, Daddy, teacher says, every time a bell rings, an angel gets his wings."

George, holding his daughter, replied, "That's right. That's right. That a boy, Clarence."

With the end of the Frank Capra film, Jennifer, who was sitting on a large couch with Stephen, looked at Zack Charmichael, whose feet were up in a recliner. "Well, Zack, what did you think?"

"I liked it. It's not what I expected. I always thought it was one of those sickly sweet holiday movies. But that was not the case at all. It had a bit of a dark edge to it."

Stephen observed, "Absolutely. But I still can't believe that this was the first time you ever saw *It's a Wonderful Life*. How did you miss seeing this Christmas classic?"

Jennifer interjected, "Stephen, didn't we settle this at dinner? Not everyone has or even wants your vast movie knowledge."

Stephen protested, "We're not talking about some obscure movie here. This time of year, how can you possibly avoid *It's a Wonderful Life*? It's everywhere."

Zack poked, "Well, maybe I had more pressing matters than to watch movies."

Stephen jobbed back, "Ah, yes, appointments with the Xbox and *Halo*."

While Stephen ranked as a big movie buff, Zack was easily Stephen's equivalent when it came to video games.

Jennifer smiled and shook her head. "Now, now, boys, play nice."

"You know we do, Jen," assured Stephen.

Jennifer got up, grabbed a couple of empty cake plates and her mug of tea. She moved from the spacious family room into the large, well-equipped kitchen. She asked, "Anyone for more dessert or tea?"

Stephen and Zack followed.

Stephen said, "I couldn't eat anything more, but I will have another tea."

Zack added, "Same here. Just another tea. Thanks."

Stephen took his mug, and picked up Jennifer's as well. "More tea, Jen?"

"No, nothing more for me. Thanks."

With two Earl Grey teas generating a waft of steam, the three caught up on some St. Mary's church business while sitting around an island bar in the middle of the kitchen. The Grant home was a Mediterranean-style structure, and Jennifer's decorating touch brought that architecture together with touches of Southwest American and Long Island by the sea. The large home, and extensive grounds for suburban Long Island, sat along an inlet that opened to Moriches Bay. The property had been in Jennifer's family for some time. After they were married, Stephen's contribution to the decor was basically limited to additional books and bookcases, and some framed classic movie posters, including one for *It's a Wonderful Life*.

Zack switched topics back to the movie. "You know, when you think about the message in *It's a Wonderful Life*, it's a powerful statement on the value of each individual human life. At its core, it's a pro-life film."

Stephen smiled and glanced at his wife.

Jennifer looked at Stephen. "It's not surprising that you two are in the same line of work." She turned to Zack. "I've heard the same thing from my husband, Zack."

Zack took a sip of tea. "I also could not help but think of what I saw on the news on Wednesday night, and what might have happened if you had not been there, Stephen."

Stephen knew this conversation was coming. Since Charmichael arrived as the assistant pastor at St. Mary's, Zack and Stephen, though separated by a decade-and-a-half in terms of age, found that they had much in common in terms of how they looked at many aspects of life, including most matters of faith and theology. They became true friends. At the same time, though, he had revealed very little of his former career to Zack. With the exception of Jennifer and fewer than a half-dozen other close friends, Stephen avoided sharing details about this part of his past. He studiously avoided, or at least tried to avoid, mixing his previous work as a SEAL and CIA with his current life as a pastor.

Given that even Jennifer had questions at breakfast yesterday, he expected inquiries from Zack, along with a few others.

Of course, that all had to happen in the middle of Sixth Avenue in Manhattan, with it inevitably being caught on video.

"Trust me, many were involved in bringing that situation under control."

Zack laughed. "Really? Come on, Stephen. You went all Jack Bauer on that guy."

"Well, I ..."

Zack's natural enthusiasm was ignited. "Hey, I'm not saying anything other than that was great." He caught himself. "I mean, you had to do what you did. Those two clowns were murdering people. But when I saw that clip, and what you did..." He shook his head in admiration, leaned back, and added, "Combine that with what I read about the shooting at St. Mary's awhile back. A few more incidents like these, and somebody's going to be making a Pastor Stephen Grant movie. Heck, maybe even a video game." Zack smiled broadly.

Jennifer said, "I'm going to cut you off right there, Pastor Charmichael, before this goes any farther down the path of fantasy, and before you pump up my husband's too-often-already-well-inflated ego."

Stephen laughed. "Hey, that was uncalled for. Besides, I think Zack's a very astute fellow."

Jennifer replied, "I'm sure you do."

Zack put his hands up in mock innocence. "Okay, it was not my intention to bring about any marital strife. And I have to get going anyway. Got to get up early."

Stephen added, "But there also might be a few friends looking to play some *Halo* on Xbox Live."

"Actually, after watching you in action, I'm feeling a little Tom Clancy-ish. Maybe *Rainbow Six*."

Chapter 32

"What the hell do the two of you want? Didn't I tell you that I would let you know when this is going to happen?" Rollin Dawes was not happy to be staring at the faces of Carter Dujas and Perry Harris on his laptop.

Dujas answered, "I know, I know, Rollin. That's what I told Perry. But he's getting nervous."

Dawes clenched his teeth. "What's your problem, Harris?"

Perry Harris looked uneasy. He shifted in his chair. "Well, um, I'm not nervous, Carter. It's just that with everything that's already happened, I was wondering if this still all makes sense. You know..."

Dawes answered, "No, Perry, I don't know. What are you talking about? We've got a mission here. Those two jack asses taken down the other day did help matters some. I'm sure they've put a little doubt in some minds about the wisdom of this public Advent prayer thing. But the news stories make clear that these two were in it for some twisted personal glory, wanting to be on television. We're going to make clear that this should be about these religious freaks sticking their noses out from under their pews. We're going to send a message that they need to get back under those pews, and stay there, forever."

Still looking uncomfortable, Harris said, "Right, right. You're absolutely correct, Rollin. Good. Good."

Dawes grunted and shook his head. "Is that it then gentlemen? I have work to do."

Dujas said, "Speaking of your work, when are you coming to New York? And do you have a team assembled? And what about the timing?"

Dawes replied, "I've been in New York, Carter, for a few days. And I've got my team. So, stop worrying. We've got some assessments to do, and then I'll let you know when this will be going down."

Dujas gave no indication that Dawes intimidated him, especially in contrast to his glaring intimidation of Harris.

Dujas said, "Good, Rollin. I actually prefer to be kept in the loop."

Dawes declared, "I'll keep both of you in the loop as is warranted." And he cut off his Internet connection.

* * *

At the same time on that Saturday afternoon, miles away in Center Moriches, on Long Island, the situation could not have been more different.

Members, choirs and leaders from seven local churches assembled on an open lawn on the corner of Main Street at the edge of the property of St. Luke's Catholic Church.

Prayers were said, Christmas hymns sung, and a large Nativity scene was assembled.

Pictures were taken, including by a reporter for a small, local weekly, who also collected quotes from priests, pastors and church members. She actually was a member of the Methodist church in attendance.

Later, all were invited into the St. Luke's School gym for coffee, tea, apple cider, and assorted pastries.

It was a joyful time of fellowship.

Stephen and Tom wandered over to Ron.

Stephen said, "See, Ron, didn't I tell you a while ago that it would all go well?"

Chapter 33

It was the second Sunday of Advent, and the evening prayers near the Christmas tree at Rockefeller Center were being hosted by a collection of traditional Anglican churches – led by the Anglican Church in North America – that had broken off from the Episcopal Church.

Through a series of calendar conflicts and late emergencies, the ACNA archbishop and the bishop of the regional diocese could not make it, so it fell to Father Tom Stone to give the evening's homily.

Of course, Maggie Stone, all of the Stone children, family, and friends – including Stephen and Jennifer Grant, Zack Charmichael and Ron McDermott – and many members of St. Bart's were on hand, among the thousand-plus in attendance.

Security was out in full force again as well.

This was the first time that Stephen was back to "An Advent for Religious Liberty" gathering since he helped stop the armored gunmen four nights earlier. He was keeping a low profile for obvious reasons. At the same time, he was not going to miss this occasion to support and listen to his good friend.

Father Stone approached the podium.

> "Grace to you and peace from God our Father and the Lord Jesus Christ.

"It's Advent. The world thinks that this is a time for shopping, parties, and yes, visiting and taking pictures of the tree right behind me.

"As long as we keep things in proper perspective, there's not necessarily anything wrong with all of this. But when it comes to our understanding of Advent as Christians now is not a time of celebration specifically. Instead, it's a period of preparation, getting ready, anticipation, waiting, and longing.

"We reflect on the Israelites' yearning and crying out to be free from slavery in Egypt.

"We think about the anticipation and preparation for the first coming of Christ. In today's Gospel lesson from Luke 3, we heard about John the Baptist telling people how to prepare for the Messiah's arrival, including repentance, a change of heart and a different way of living.

"And of course, we look ahead. We are to get ready, waiting and longing for Christ's Second Coming. We await the Prince of Peace.

"This time of Advent, then, also reminds the Christian of our responsibilities as we await that Second Coming. Those responsibilities include helping the poor, the sick, the abused, and so many others. That is, to care for our fellow man.

"Ultimately, we have a duty to spread the Good News of forgiveness, love, redemption and salvation through Jesus Christ.

"In order to do that, of course, we must be out in the world, just as we are here tonight.

"We are literally on the streets of New York City tonight for 'An Advent for Religious Liberty.' The Mayor-elect of this great city has declared a political war on religion, especially, it seems, on Christians. He wishes to ban us from public life, as well as repeating the lie that the Catholic Church is a hate group. And by the way, for those of us who are not Catholics, rest assured that if this outrageous charge goes unanswered, all of us will be added to this list of hate groups by Mr. Pritchett and his friends.

"Others in the political world, of course, also have pushed to force various church institutions to violate their core beliefs or abandon many of the good works they do in the world.

"So, in this 'Advent for Religious Liberty,' we prepare and await deliverance, and that deliverance comes via the strength and purpose provided by the Holy Spirit, from which we act to defend our faith against violation and oppression.

"The irony is rich, my brothers and sisters. For as Mr. Pritchett seeks to limit our voices in the public square, here we are in the public square, speaking out louder than ever in defense of the liberty of the Christian, as well as in defense of the liberty of all other people of faith. Fellow Christians are doing this across the nation, and even in other countries.

"I think of what St. Paul wrote in Romans 5: '[W]e rejoice in our sufferings, knowing that suffering produces endurance, and endurance produces character, and character produces hope, and hope does not put us to shame, because God's love has been poured into our hearts through the Holy Spirit who has been given to us.'

> "Endure. Stay strong in character. And bask in God's love. I thank God for each of you, and ask His blessing upon each of you. Amen."

As the crowd later dispersed, a television reporter spotted Mike Vanacore and Melissa Ambler lingering, arm in arm. The woman swept in with a microphone, and a cameraman in tow.

"Mr. Vanacore, Ms. Ambler, it's interesting to see you here. Do you mind a quick interview?"

Mike and Mel looked at each other, shrugged their shoulders, and together said, "Sure."

The camera light clicked on, and the reporter said, "Video game entrepreneur Mike Vanacore and supermodel Melissa Ambler, it's wonderful to see you both here. I have two questions to ask. First, there have been rumors, so, are you two officially a couple?"

Melissa smiled, revealing perfect, bright white teeth. "Happily, I guess the answer to that is yes." She squeezed Mike's arm.

Vanacore added, "I can't figure out exactly why this special, beautiful woman agreed to go out with me, a tech nerd, but yes, we've been dating for a while now."

The reporter's voice then ticked down an octave. "Some might be surprised to see the two of you at this event. Why are you here?"

Mike started to open his mouth, but Melissa spoke first. "Our Christian beliefs are central to both of us. They helped create the people we are today." She looked at Mike, and asked, "Right?"

He smiled back with a look of infatuation. "Absolutely."

Melissa continued, "So, it's hard to think of something more important than this right now. How can religious liberty be under attack in this country? And elected officials labeling a church that helps so many a hate group?

I just don't get it. Given all of this, we needed to be here, and hope that others will stand up with us."

The reporter turned to Vanacore. "Mike?"

"I can't add to that. Mel put it nicely."

Meanwhile, several paces away, the Stone family and other friends were amiably chatting on the corner of 49th Street and Rockefeller Plaza. The main topic eventually came down to whether or not late dinner and drinks were in order in the city, or should they just head back to Long Island for the night.

Before a decision was finalized, a woman with blond hair framing a round face said, "Excuse me, Father Stone?"

Tom turned around. "Yes?"

He shook her hand.

"My name is Maureen Donahue. I just wanted to thank you for your sermon tonight. It helped me gain some clarity about Advent, and what it means."

"You're welcome, Ms. Donahue. I'm glad I helped at least one person tonight." He smiled.

She shifted uncomfortably, looking down at the ground and then back at Stone. "Yes, you did. I, um, well ... thank you, again."

Tom asked, "Are you alright? Was there something else that I can help with?"

"I don't want to bother you."

Tom guided her a few feet away from the group. "Maureen, is it?"

She nodded.

"Maureen, it's no bother. It's part of the job description to see if I can help."

"I don't know why I'm telling you this, but I don't have too many people that I can talk about this with face to face. Until a few days ago, I was an aide to Adam Pritchett. Actually, I was his press secretary."

"Really? What happened?"

"Well, once he handed me that statement on the crazy idea that the Catholic Church is a hate group, I quit."

Tom smiled. "Good for you, Maureen."

"Thanks, I think. But I've been kind of lost since then. My parents have been great. But they're not around here. And all of my friends are in politics. And well, I feel..."

"A bit lost? Out of place? Unsure as to what's next?"

Maureen smiled a bit. "That's pretty much it. Yes."

"Well, if you need someone to talk with, these people never shut up." He pointed her back to the Stone group.

"Oh no, I couldn't intrude."

"Stop. The more the merrier." Tom announced to the group, "Everyone, this is Maureen Donahue. By the way, she is my new hero. She was Adam Pritchett's press secretary, but quit when she found out that he was declaring political war on the Catholic Church."

A few cheers, along with smiles, handshakes, and introductions, greeted Maureen.

Tom asked, "So, have we decided what we're doing, where we're going?"

Mike and Melissa returned from their brief interview. Vanacore announced, "Well, I took the liberty of reserving the second floor of a nice little restaurant over on Seventh. Food and drink await all of us."

The appreciative group followed Mike Vanacore, with Maureen swept along as well.

Chapter 34

"These religious nuts are getting on my nerves," declared Adam Pritchett, as he tossed aside the *Daily News*, which highlighted Tom Stone's sermon.

The reporter took particular notice of, and apparent delight in, Stone's ironic point. The quote from his sermon was blown up on page 3: "For as Mr. Pritchett seeks to limit our voices in the public square, here we are in the public square, speaking out louder than ever in defense of the liberty of the Christian, as well as in defense of the liberty of all other people of faith."

The media continued their vendetta against Pritchett. They actually were feeding the religious fires against the incoming mayor.

Pritchett's anger on this Monday morning was mounting by the second. "Something needs to take these people down! Teach them a lesson that will not soon be forgotten."

Listening to the latest rant were both Carter Dujas and Dean Havenport, seated across from Pritchett's large U-desk.

Dujas added, "We can only hope. You never know."

While Pritchett continued to storm about his office, it was clear that he was not listening to his employee. But Havenport was zeroed in on Dujas.

Havenport said, “If only that were the case. But it would have to be a real, hard lesson, with an unmistakable message. Not like those random gunmen.”

Dujas smiled ever so slightly, and nodded in agreement to Havenport.

After the rant was over, Pritchett sent both Dujas and Havenport out of his office. The Mayor-elect was ready to fire off another press statement, expanding his attack to include the comments made by Father Tom Stone.

Dujas invited Havenport into his office, and closed the door.

They sat from across each other at Dujas’s desk.

Dujas said, “How serious were you in there, Dean?”

“Very much, Carter. I’ve had enough of this crap from the Religious Right. And this point yesterday, from some asshole priest, just makes Adam and the rest of us look weak. Excuse the pun, but they need the fear of no God put in them.”

“I couldn’t agree more. You didn’t hear it from me, and I know you’ll not let this go outside this office, but there’s information around that we just might get our wish, perhaps tonight.”

Dujas smiled darkly.

Chapter 35

When Rich Noack heard from Dean Havenport, the FBI already had Rollin Dawes and three members of his team – Sam Lindell, Wanda Barletta, and Nate Weiner – under surveillance.

When his planning began, Dawes had rented a recently erected, pre-fab, mini-warehouse on Jericho Turnpike in Syosset on Long Island. The facility was set well back, with a small sandwich shop providing a shield between it and the busy, four-lane road. At the same time, there was immediate access to the Long Island Expressway, and eventually three bridges and two tunnels providing access to Manhattan.

As four armed and armored FBI teams surrounded the warehouse at 10:25 AM, the only person missing was Ned Jennings.

The FBI teams, led by Noack and Trent Nguyen, secured and cleared the immediate surrounding area smoothly, quietly and quickly, with Nassau County Police moving in to stop traffic.

There were three ways in and out of the building – a front door, a garage door in the front as well, and a backdoor.

Noack radioed all team members. "Final reminder, people. As far as we know, there are four in there. Extremely dangerous. We assume heavily armed, including the possibility of explosives. Two vans. If anyone so much as breathes the wrong way once we are in, we take no chances. God's speed everyone. We move on my mark. Three, two, one, mark!"

For all of his planning as to how the attack on the Christians on 48th Street in Manhattan would take place, it apparently never crossed the mind of Rollin Dawes that law enforcement might come sweeping in on his own warehouse. There was no lookout.

Barletta and Lindell worked attaching detonators to blocks of C4. Weiner loaded those explosives, along with Russian-made RGD-5 blast and fragmentation hand grenades, into boxes labeled fresh seafood, then spread trays of actual seafood over the C4 and grenades, and sealed each box. In turn, Dawes moved the boxes into the vans. Each van had colorful lettering, advertising a nonexistent seafood company from Long Island.

The only real preparation for the forthcoming assault for Dawes and his team was the lingering paranoia that kept submachine guns within arms reach.

Noack's team of six led the way to the front door, while Nguyen's was first to the backdoor. Battering rams tore the front and back doors from their hinges, followed by shouts of "FBI" and "Hands where we can see them."

But the response was weapons fire from Barletta, Lindell and Weiner. Dawes leaped into the back of a van, and scrambled across the fresh seafood, grenades and C4.

Lindell took a bullet to the head, and was dead before hitting the ground.

But Barletta and Weiner continued firing. Barletta squeezed off rounds from behind the table of explosives, while Weiner found cover with one of the open doors of the other van.

As shooting continued, Dawes crawled behind the driver's seat of the van.

Barletta grabbed a grenade from the table, pulled the pin and moved to throw it in the direction of Noack's team. From the other direction, though, Trent Nguyen fired three rounds from his Glock 22. Barletta's toss went astray when two of Nguyen's bullets hit her chest, with one stopping her heart from beating.

The grenade landed by the garage door, and blew it halfway off its track.

Dawes reacted by moving into the driver's seat, starting the van, slipping the vehicle into drive, and hitting the gas. The van's engine strained to react to the signal being sent via the accelerator hitting the floor.

Dawes pointed his Uzi SMG out the window, and sprayed bullets in all directions while the van moved forward. Most of the FBI agents jumped out of the way. One was hit by a grazing shot on his cheek.

But as he saw the van moving away from him to the partially open bay door, Nguyen immediately holstered his gun and ran after the vehicle.

Weiner stopped firing for an ever-so-brief moment to watch the van moving out, and cursed. In that moment when Weiner's guard fell, Rich Noack, amidst the chaos around him, took a deep breath, steadied his own Glock, and fired off two rounds. Like Lindell, Weiner was dead before his body came to rest on the concrete floor.

As the van struck and plowed through the partially attached garage door, Nguyen lunged and grabbed hold of the open, swinging backdoor of the van.

As Dawes moved the vehicle from side to side, Nguyen struggled to hang on.

As he bounced the van out onto Jericho Turnpike, Dawes withdrew his weapon from the window, and tossed it onto the seat next to him. He then braked and whipped the steering wheel to the left. The backdoor swung fully open, with Nguyen dragging his feet on the tar of the road. Coming out of the skid, the door swung back, and with the van in a virtually stopped position for a split second, Nguyen pushed with his legs, let go of the door, and managed to get most of his body into the back of the vehicle.

Dawes hit the gas pedal, which threw Nguyen off again, as the boxes of fish and explosives he was laying on started moving out the back of the van.

For good measure, Dawes finally spotted his uninvited passenger.

Dawes sped at three police cars blocking the street, with the eastbound lanes beyond them backed up with traffic. He targeted the space between the two cars blocking the westbound side.

Nguyen had managed to stop himself from slipping out the back and onto the road. But Dawes was reaching across to the passenger seat for his Uzi. As he pulled the weapon up and started aiming it at his passenger, Nguyen used his legs one more time to hurl his body forward.

The FBI agent came over the back of the driver's seat, and crashed into Dawes, driving the man's head hard into the steering wheel. The submachine gun fell out of Dawes' hand. But control over the van was lost as well. The steering wheel was pushed sharply, which resulted in the van turning hard right. The vehicle tipped, and began to roll over.

On the second flip, Dawes' head slipped just outside the driver side window, and as the weight of the flipping van came down, his neck snapped and skull was partially crushed.

The van stopped its roll by crashing into a police car.

Despite his large, six-foot-six frame, and being the oldest agent on the scene, Noack was the first to get to the van. With the vehicle on its side, Noack used the undercarriage to climb up, and stuck his bald head inside the passenger side door.

Looking inside, he saw blood, and the head of Rollin Dawes resting in an unnatural position.

Noack yelled, "Trent! Trent, are you okay? Can you hear me?"

Dawes dead body began to move, as a groan came from below.

Nguyen managed to declare, "Fine, Rich. I think. Somebody get this dead son of a bitch off me, and get me the hell out of here."

* * *

When the FBI was about to move in on the pre-fab warehouse, about a mile or so east on the same road, Lt. Mel Dwyer of the Nassau County Police was in a 7-Eleven pouring a cup of pumpkin spice coffee.

He was supposed to be off today, but was heading into work with the sudden FBI activity.

As he pushed a lid on the coffee, a man stepped up next to him, and tapped into the pumpkin spice coffee as well.

Dwyer, still looking down at his cup, smiled and said, "I have to admit, I can't get enough of that stuff. My co-workers mock me ruthlessly."

The man laughed. "Yeah, me too. If the guys I'm working with knew that I was stopping here to get pumpkin spice coffee, I'd be dead."

Dwyer finally looked at the man, and raised an eyebrow. "Enjoy the coffee and your day."

"You, too," answered the man.

Dwyer dropped more than enough cash for the coffee on the counter. He told the clerk, "Keep the change." And he exited the convenience store quickly.

Dwyer's fellow pumpkin spice coffee fan was not moving as fast. He grabbed a buttered roll, paid for his items, asked for a few extra napkins, and left.

As he approached his car, parked at the end of the building, around the corner came Dwyer with his gun drawn. “Ned Jennings, drop the bag and, I hate to say this, toss aside the pumpkin spice coffee as well. You’re under arrest. Hands on the car.”

Chapter 36

Five FBI agents had arrived at the offices of Pritchett NYC Enterprises at the same time the teams were arriving at the warehouse on Long Island.

One agent remained at the bank of elevators, and another at the emergency staircase exit.

But the primary person they sought, Carter Dujas, was not around. His administrative assistant seemed bewildered, telling the FBI that he certainly had been in earlier. Now, she didn't know where he had gone.

Adam Pritchett arrived at the scene. "What's the meaning of this?"

Special Agent John Smith showed his credentials, and informed Pritchett that they were looking for Dujas. Rather than answering Pritchett's question as to why Dujas was being sought, Smith informed Pritchett that the staff would be individually interviewed this afternoon.

Smith added, "And that includes you, Mr. Mayor-elect, especially in light of that press statement you put out early today."

Pritchett's statement reiterated much of what he had said before on the matter of religion in public life. But this time, he added a closing sentence: "A presumptive arrogance came from this religious gathering on Sunday night that cries out for a lesson to be taught. That lesson will come through loud and clear when I take office."

Smith coolly ignored Pritchett's protests, and asked to be directed to Dean Havenport's office.

Pritchett grunted. "Follow me."

They arrived at a closed door on the other side of the floor. Pritchett opened without knocking, and then came up short. "Oh, my God. What the hell? Dean..."

Dean Havenport was slumped back in his office chair. His once white shirt was drenched in dark red due to blood that had flown forth from six gunshot wounds in his chest and stomach.

Agent Smith walked over to the body. He looked at the other two agents in the room. "No one leaves, obviously. Call this in, and have them relay the information to NYPD. Make sure everyone is looking for Carter Dujas."

Chapter 37

By late Monday afternoon, Cardinal Capriano had received calls from Mayor Richardson, the police commissioner, and FBI Supervisory Special Agent Rich Noack urging him to put an end to "An Advent for Religious Liberty."

The message basically was the same from each: It was just too dangerous to continue, and besides, the point had been made, right?

He flipped through the old-school Rolodex on his desk, stopped at a number, picked up his phone and dialed.

At St. Mary's Lutheran Church, Barbara Tunney stuck her head inside Pastor Stephen Grant's office door. "There's a call for you on Line 1."

Grant had the television on in his office, with a local reporter going over the developments in Nassau County earlier in the afternoon. "Who is it, Barb?"

She raised an eyebrow. "Cardinal Capriano."

Stephen clicked off the television, and said, "Really? Thanks."

He picked up. "Cardinal Capriano, how are you?"

"Given everything that's been happening, Pastor Grant, I'm not sure."

"That's certainly understandable. How can I help?"

"You've already been a tremendous help, of course. What you had to do to stop those gunmen, and your wisdom in sending Ms. Caldwell and her team our way – that's all much appreciated. But now, I need some advice, and you're the only person that I know who can see the entire picture, I think."

"What is it?"

"I've gotten calls today from various people in power, urging me to stop this 'Advent for Religious Liberty.' They worry, as we all do, about additional violence. You are one of the few people with expertise, if you will, that can address both sides of this. Both as a pastor and with your military and intelligence background. What do you think?"

Just a small matter. No pressure.

"Well, it's not an easy call. And I would understand if you chose to cancel the rest of this. But I certainly wouldn't cancel. This is a critical time for Christians in this country to show clear and complete commitment in standing up for what we believe and to make clear that we have every right to say what we believe to the world. We cannot afford to step back in the face of whatever challenge is put in our path. After all, what did our Lord and Savior go through for each one of us? As for the security side, madmen or zealots can strike at any time. It's up to the police and FBI, in these cases, to do their jobs in protecting the public. And what they accomplished today, to take down a group before it struck, speaks volumes about their abilities. Believe me, that happens with the FBI and CIA, for example, more than the public ever imagines. But as we've learned before, as good as we might be, the crazies only need to be lucky once."

Cardinal Capriano said, "Thank you, Pastor Grant. Your candor is much appreciated. And just so you know, you reinforced exactly what I was thinking."

Chapter 38

By Wednesday morning, the degree of opposition to Pritchett had reached previously unfathomable levels.

The media was nearly unanimous in calling for him to step aside even before taking office as mayor. Speculation was rampant as to what role Pritchett might have played in the murder of Havenport, his possible affiliation with the group taken down in Nassau County, and with his close aide, Carter Dujas, who apparently was on the lam. It was an unimaginable field day for reporters and commentators.

Even the most supportive of Pritchett's fellow Democrats abandoned him. That included State Assemblyman Blair Quinton, who now said, "Pritchett's not doing anyone any good by hanging around. He's in deep trouble, and certainly not helping those of us who take the separation of church and state, the separation of church and public life seriously. We can't let this man take office as mayor."

Suddenly, New Yorkers learned that the New York City Charter allowed for a mayor to be removed from office by the governor. However, there was nothing, apparently, to do about a mayor-elect.

As for Adam Pritchett, he sat in his office, quietly staring at a newsfeed on a computer screen.

Pritchett had ordered his assistant, Erin, to tell all inquirers that he would not be speaking with them. But she was to provide him every couple of hours with an updated list of media who had called.

He clicked on a live discussion between three city political reporters.

One reporter declared, "Listen, we were used to this guy not talking to reporters during his campaign. We just thought he was incredibly arrogant. We've since discovered that when he does talk, or issue press statements, he only gets himself in deeper trouble. His silence before with the media apparently wasn't about arrogance. It was about stupidity, or given the latest news, something dire or dangerous, with some stupid sprinkled in as well."

Pritchett sprang to his feet, grabbed the computer monitor, ripped it loose from cords, moved from behind his desk, and hurled it at the floor-to-ceiling windows looking down on Fifth Avenue. The screen crashed against the window, yet it left the thick, tempered, laminated glass seemingly unaffected.

The door burst open, and a panicky Erin asked, "Mr. Pritchett, what happened? Are you alright?"

Pritchett was unmoving, now standing at the window, staring out across the metropolis. "I'm fine, Erin. Please get someone from tech in here to clean this up, and install a new screen."

Chapter 39

The next few days passed without incident. Investigations proceeded. Much of the nation watched the latest news from New York, while also shopping for Christmas presents.

The weather turned dramatically colder, and television weather prognosticators spoke of an increasing chance for a major snowstorm on Christmas Eve.

It was the Fourth Sunday of Advent, and after the Hymn of the Day, Stephen spoke from the pulpit at St. Mary's.

> "We heard from Moses today in Deuteronomy. He noted that the Lord said, 'I will raise up for them a prophet like you from among their brothers. And I will put my words in his mouth, and he shall speak to them all that I command him.'
>
> "As this Advent soon comes to a close on Christmas Eve, it serves us well to consider these, as well as other commands from God, to speak out, in particular, to share His word.
>
> "We have a responsibility to spread the Gospel to all corners of the world.
>
> "When it comes to the political arena, though, I'm in the camp that pastors, church

leaders and entire denominations should be very careful when they venture out to take stands on political issues.

"When no biblical or moral imperative exists, churches should leave it to the freedom of the Christian in their roles as citizens, acting according to a morally informed conscience, to make the best decisions they can. Otherwise, when church leaders take stands on these kinds of issues, it only creates further division within the Church. There are seemingly countless issues in the political arena that we can and do disagree on, and that does not diminish any of us as faithful Christians.

"But, of course, there are times when our faith requires that we take a stand. That is, if we do not speak out, we are not doing what God asks of us. The most obvious are cases of protecting innocent human life, from conception to death; protecting the institution of marriage as being between a man and a woman as God has proclaimed through both Holy Scripture and His natural law; and standing against any kind of genocide and other glaring evils.

"While far from perfect – indeed, the Church is not immune from man's sinful nature – Christians often have been and are voices for what is right and just.

"That being the case, this is why I have been truly frightened by the recent efforts, as manifested by New York City Mayor-elect Pritchett, to in effect silence Christianity in the public arena. That was followed closely by the attempt to label our fellow Christians in the Catholic Church as a hate group.

"In a land founded in part on the promise of religious liberty, this often seems unbelievable. With the very First Amendment to our Constitution beginning, 'Congress shall make no law respecting an establishment of religion, or prohibiting the free exercise thereof,' it is incomprehensible that we have gotten to this point.

"Yet here we are in a position whereby we must declare this to be 'An Advent for Religious Liberty.' It is a time in which we prepare and await a return to a proper civic understanding, a proper constitutional understanding, and a proper respect for religious liberty.

"As many of you know, I'm not only your pastor, but something of a history buff as well. No respected historian would ever say that the First Amendment was meant for there to be a wall of separation between church and state so that the church should be silent on matters involving the state, or silent in our broad public, community life together. Quite the contrary, the First Amendment protects the full and free exercise of religion.

"In fact, it's amazing how the meaning of Thomas Jefferson's letter, from which the expression 'a wall of separation between Church and State' comes, has been turned on its head. Jefferson was responding to and agreeing with a letter sent by the Danbury Baptist Association. The point of the association's letter was that government should not infringe upon one's religious beliefs.

"The association's letter said: 'Our sentiments are uniformly on the side of religious liberty: that Religion is at all times and places a matter between God and individuals, that no man ought to suffer in name, person, or effects on account of his religious opinions, [and] that the legitimate power of civil government extends no further than to punish the man who works ill to his neighbor.'

"Jefferson was agreeing with these points. He clearly was not making a case for there being no links or interaction between religion and government. In the end, the point of the First Amendment was to make sure that government did not create an official church, since so many who came here fled a state church, and that the state could not limit the freedom of religion.

"But in various ways over recent decades, many in politics have sought to limit religious freedom through a gross misinterpretation of this phrase that does not appear in our Constitution.

"Adam Pritchett's declaration and intentions on this front actually amount to nothing more than the natural step forward for these forces. And yes, we have an obligation to speak out against such a gross infringement of religious liberty. As someone recently said to me: We would be negligent if we did not act.

"Later today, I hope most of you will be joining us on the bus ride into the city as our own Lutheran Church will lead tonight's prayers during the 'Advent of Religious Liberty.'

"And let us pray for our nation in these troubling times."

In the late afternoon, two buses filled with members of St. Mary's Lutheran Church parked in a lot on the west side of Manhattan that had been reserved for such vehicles throughout "An Advent for Religious Liberty."

On the side of each bus, signs were secured saying, "St. Mary's Lutheran Supports Religious Liberty."

Parked next to those two large buses was a mini-bus, with darkened windows and no markings. Fifteen people got out. They were dressed, deceptively and purposefully, in the style of Mennonites – the men in overalls, simple coats and straw hats, with the women in plain dresses and coats, with bonnets on their heads. Fourteen clustered closely around the leader like they were praying. They listened to his instructions. He declared in a low voice, "We're only going to practice 'A' tonight for obvious reasons at the vigil. Later, we will go by the Pritchett Building and then City Hall. We'll discuss all of the options and formations we might need to carry out for each location. Don't worry, brothers and sisters, Pritchett will have some public event at his building or at City Hall, or given his arrogance, even confront this Advent gathering head on, in person. Wherever he appears, we will act. Our dress is perfect. We stand out, but in a way that will never draw suspicion. We only need to be ready when opportunity comes from above."

They followed him closely, walking across town to the Advent gathering.

As the St. Mary's group exited their two buses, Stephen noticed the plainly dressed group. *Haven't seen any Mennonites until now. Certainly stand out in New York City.*

Once they were in the crowd, the leader simply said "A," and they separated, and moved among those gathered. Their eyes darted from person to person.

None were listening to a powerful message about how the birth and, yes, suffering, death, and resurrection of

Chapter 40

Noack pushed his chair back from a conference room table that was covered in files, paper, coffee cups, and a few open laptops. "Unless I'm missing something here, people, despite what it looks like at first blush, I don't think Pritchett was in on or knew about any of this. Am I wrong?"

The five other FBI agents in the room, including Agents Nguyen and Smith, offered nothing to counter the statement.

Nguyen reaffirmed, "When you look at what Perry Harris confessed to and reported about his conversations with Dawes and Dujas, what Dean Havenport relayed before his murder, and Pritchett's own reactions when finding Havenport dead and his answers to our questioning, I think its hard to make a case against Pritchett."

Of course, FBI agents were not immune to the dynamics of bureaucratic meetings. Others in the room started echoing the same ideas, just restating them in different fashion. Noack quickly shut that down, however.

"Okay, we still have things to wrap up on this regarding Pritchett, in order to hand it over to the attorney general's office. If everything else checks out, they'll want to get this out, to remove it as any kind of political football." He switched gears. "Far more important, though, is to track down Dujas. Do we have anything else on his whereabouts?"

Smith spoke up in a monotone voice, "I hate to say it, but it's like the guy just disappeared. We've found nothing on him since he left the Pritchett offices."

Noack shut the file on the table in front of him. "He's the main priority. We need to find Dujas. Get to it, people. And thanks for all your work."

Chapter 41

Snow, certainly at any real depth, was rare in New York City at Christmas time. But the predictions for this Christmas Eve day and night were for steady, slowly accumulating snow.

This pleased Stephen and Jennifer Grant.

Stephen noticed that Jennifer seemed to get romantic notions whenever it snowed. She spoke regretfully about missing snow when growing up in Las Vegas. When flakes fell around or on Christmas Eve, her delight only seemed magnified.

This was the oddest schedule for a Christmas Eve Stephen had since becoming a pastor. It was the last night for "An Advent for Religious Liberty," and he was expected to be there. That left Zack on his own at St. Mary's to cover the three Christmas Eve services.

Stephen pledged to take all of the Confirmation classes through their conclusion in May, four months beyond the January responsibilities he already acquired due to their football wager. Zack protested, but when Stephen persisted, those protests ceased rather quickly.

A few families from St. Mary's were making the journey into the city for this final night's prayers. They and a wide assortment of other Lutherans gathered for a late afternoon Christmas Eve service at St. John's Lutheran Cathedral.

Pastor Bruce Ericsson's joy at having a nearly full Christmas Eve service in this gothic, mini-cathedral was evident. As the service proceeded, Stephen watched his fellow clergy member. *Enjoy, Bruce. Most of the world outside doesn't understand why we get so happy when our churches are full. The Word. The Sacrament. Coming together to worship the Lord, and to support and love each other. If only this were true each week, right?*

It was a fairly long walk from St. John's over to the Rockefeller Center tree. But since they had the time, Stephen and Jennifer decided to make the journey on foot. Arms interlocked, they talked, laughed and peeked in the windows of a few stores as the snow came down.

The route they chose eventually took them by the front doors of St. Patrick's Cathedral. When stopped briefly to look up at the combination of church spires, skyscrapers, city lights and snowflakes, a voice called out, "Pastor Grant? Jennifer?"

They turned their heads in unison to see Maureen Donahue bouncing down the steps of St. Patrick's. The three had met just two nights earlier when Father Stone had given the homily on 48th Street. They sat together at the late dinner afterwards hosted by Mike Vanacore.

Maureen was beaming. "Hello. Wasn't that a wonderful reading in church?" She stopped, scrunched her face a bit apparently trying to recall it. "Therefore the Lord himself will give you a sign. Behold, a ... no, wait ... the virgin shall conceive and bear a son, and shall call his name Immanuel."

Stephen smiled, "Yes. Isaiah 7:14."

Maureen said, "These last two days have been great. What a change. I don't think I've ever felt so ... well ... energized coming out of Mass. Are you going to the prayer vigil?"

Jennifer answered, "Absolutely. Why don't you come with us?'

Maureen said, "Great. I'd love to."

They arrived early, but the NYPD already had shut down that part of 48th Street to vehicular traffic for the Christmas Eve gathering.

After just a few minutes, Stephen spotted Father Ron McDermott.

Maureen and Ron were introduced and greetings of "Merry Christmas" were exchanged.

Stephen asked Ron, "How'd you get away from St. Luke's for tonight?"

"Father Burns can't stay away. He's back for a visit already, and insisted that I come here. I'm not sure, but given the reaction to his visit, I don't think anyone's going to miss me tonight." Father Stanley Burns had been the longtime senior parish priest at St. Luke's Roman Catholic Church and School, and had just recently retired.

Stephen knew that Ron was simply exhibiting his expressionless, dry humor. But he appreciated Jen's impulse to respond.

She said, "Ron, I know that's not the case. Your parishioners love their priest."

Stephen's cellphone rumbled in his pocket. He looked at the screen and saw Brett Matthews' name and number.

"Brett, hello. Where are you?"

Dr. Matthews replied, "I'm behind the stage, and your presence is required."

"Why?"

"Tonight's going to run a little differently. Cardinal Capriano wants various Christian leaders on the stage in a final show of unity."

"Makes sense, but what does that have to do with me? I thought you just wanted me around to help behind the scenes, if needed, and to provide another set of eyes on the event."

"All of that's true. But the Cardinal also wants you on stage. He's not going to announce your role with the gunmen, though everyone already knows, obviously, but he insists that key people in this entire Advent and religious liberty effort at least be on stage. Besides, won't that give you a better view to keep an eye on things?"

That last point is a good one.

Stephen said, "Okay, I'll be around to you shortly." He put the phone away, and turned to Jennifer. "I've been summoned to be on stage. Do you mind?"

"Mind?" she replied. "Of course not. Go do what you do."

They exchanged a quick kiss.

Stephen asked Ron, "Can I trust you to watch over the ladies?"

Jennifer interrupted in mock protest. "Excuse me?" Stephen winked at her.

Ron smiled and nodded. "At your service, as always, my friend."

Within an hour, after nearly everyone gathered had sung, "O Come, O Come, Emmanuel," Francis Cardinal Capriano stepped up to the microphone.

There was barely enough room on the stage for everyone that Capriano wanted up there. Grant was more than happy to be in the back. But being a bit taller than most and positioning himself in the right spot, he could still see into much of the crowd.

The Cardinal opened with a blessing, and then said, "Let's listen to a reading from Luke, perhaps the most beloved reading for Christmas: 'And in the same region there were shepherds out in the field, keeping watch over their flock by night. And an angel of the Lord appeared to them, and they were filled with fear.'"

When he started reading, the hush of the crowd, combined with the snowfall, created an unusual silence. But some stirring began to the left, and moved closer to the stage.

Capriano continued, "'And the angel said to them, "Fear not, for behold, I bring you good news of great joy that will be for all people.'"

The disturbance increased and approached the stage.

"'"For unto you is born this day in the city of David a Savior, who is Christ the Lord."'"

Capriano glanced up to see Adam Pritchett, accompanied by four of his personal security guards, standing on the ground in front of him. The Cardinal met Pritchett's stare and continued from memory, "'"And this will be a sign for you: you will find a baby wrapped in swaddling cloths and lying in a manger." And suddenly there was with the angel a multitude of the heavenly host praising God and saying, "Glory to God in the highest, and on earth peace among those with whom he is pleased!"'"

Lee Morrison and his 14 followers were in a group roughly 20 yards in front of the stage. Morrison's eyes bored in on Pritchett.

From their separate perches above 48th, Paige Caldwell and Sean McEnany watched. Paige said into her two-way radio earpiece, "Are you seeing this, Sean?"

"I am," he answered from the other end of the block.

They both shifted to continue watching through the scopes on their rifles.

On the ground, Trent Nguyen began moving closer to the stage from the west, and Rich Noack did the same from the east.

On one side of the head of the Baptist preacher in front of him, Grant could see the face of Pritchett looking up. He had no read on the man. Shifting to the other side, Grant could only see the back of Capriano's head. *None of this is helping.*

After reading the words about peace, Capriano's face broke into a broad smile, and with open arms, he motioned that Pritchett should join him on stage.

The Mayor-elect's expression did not change, but he worked his way to the stairs, climbed them, and walked past amazed faces on stage to reach out and shake Capriano's hand.

Pritchett leaned in to Capriano, and whispered, "We need to come to an understanding. Might I say a brief word?"

With Capriano now faced in his direction, Grant could see a look of complete surprise on the Cardinal's face.

Capriano whispered back, "I am here with open arms, and trust. I hope that is not misplaced. Please, go ahead."

As snowflakes began to gather on Pritchett's unkempt gray hair and create water drops on his glasses, he spoke to a crowd whose silence now hung precariously in the air. "It is unfortunate that this political disagreement has spilled into the streets of Manhattan as it has over these past few weeks."

Murmurings started to cut the silence.

"I just wanted to say that, while I disagree with everything you stand for, I am not an enemy of religion."

Grumbling in the crowd grew, with a few boos ringing out.

Grant felt a red alert beginning. *What is he doing? This guy is incredibly clueless.* He slipped his way past a few people in front of him, who seemed to not care as they were focused on Pritchett standing right in front of them. Grant's focus, however, moved to scanning the crowd.

Pritchett continued, "My intention is not to ban religion from our city, but merely to keep it in its proper place."

The crowd's disagreement expanded in scope and volume. Cardinal Capriano shook his head. His smile of a few moments ago had melted completely into a grim look. He took two steps closer to Pritchett.

On the ground, Lee Morrison turned to his followers, and through gritted teeth, he whispered, "God has delivered the evildoer into our midst. He is good and we are blessed. Brothers and sisters, execute plan B."

Morrison turned back at the stage, and the other 14 formed a circle with their backs to the middle. The men reached inside their overalls, and the women inside the small, plain bags they carried. Each removed a small revolver.

From the stage, Grant saw the glint of a gun barrel raised. As he darted to Pritchett and Capriano, he screamed, "Gun, get down!"

He angled himself so that his lunge should push down both Pritchett and the Cardinal. No one else was moving when Grant left the ground. As Morrison fired, Grant hit Pritchett who dominoed into Capriano, and they both hit the stage floor, with Capriano then toppling off to the ground some ten feet below.

Havoc reigned.

All 14 members of Morrison's group fired into the people around them.

Maureen Donahue saw the guns just a few feet away, and she yelled at Jennifer, "Look out!" As shots rang out, Donahue grabbed Jennifer and pulled her down to the ground. Ron turned to see the two women hit the road below, and he dove on top, spreading out his body over the two as protection.

People screamed in pain and fear, desperately moving away from this circle of death.

McEnany reported, "Front of the stage. Twenty or so yards in front. They're in a fucking circle and shooting."

Caldwell coolly replied, "Got them."

The fact that the group remained in one place, and the intended victims were moving away, presented relatively clear shots.

Caldwell squeezed, and one of the women shooters fell. McEnany hit another with a headshot, leaving little of the man's skull intact.

When those two fell, a dozen of the others started whirling around in place, looking for those returning fire. Morrison, though, broke for the stage.

McEnany said, "Good. They're panicked. Stopped shooting civilians, looking for us. Too damn bad, assholes. You won't find us."

He fired off another round, and another murderer fell to the ground.

Caldwell did not speak. She trained the rifle through the scope, and fired off two shots in quick succession. Each one hit home. An FBI sniper got another.

On the street level, Noack and Nguyen moved against the Christians moving away in fear. Noack used the power of his large body to get free first. He then stopped, trained his Glock on one of the shooters who was looking at the buildings above, fired off two shots, and down the man went.

Nguyen never stopped once free of the crowd. He fired on the run. Two more of the terrorists fell as a result. But the remaining three now found someone at which they could return fire. Each got off a shot that missed Nguyen, and those would be their last rounds.

One took a slug in the back from Noack, and the other two died as bullets descended from different directions and different windows above the street.

* * *

While FBI Agent Nguyen was moving into the open, Lee Morrison was climbing the stairs and moving across the stage.

Grant had gotten back on his feet, and suddenly found himself between a man approaching with a gun and the next mayor of New York.

Morrison shouted, "Get out of the way!"

Where's my freakin' gun when I need it most?

Grant responded, "I can't do that. Why don't we...?"

Morrison fired, hitting Grant, who fell back on the floor at the feet of Adam Pritchett.

Caldwell saw Grant get hit, and yelled, "No! You son of a bitch."

Pritchett pleaded, "Please, don't."

Morrison laughed, "Oh, really? Sorry, but evil like you must be wiped from this earth, Mr. Mayor."

But his laughter was cut short, as a large caliber bullet entered his forehead, courtesy of Paige Caldwell.

* * *

When the shooting stopped, Ron looked around and moved off of the two women.

"Jen, Maureen, are you alright?"

Maureen rolled over, and groaned lowly.

Jennifer bolted up. "I'm fine, Ron. Stephen? Where is he?"

He replied, "Go. Find him. I'll see to Maureen."

Jennifer looked up to the stage, and ran to the stairs.

She passed people checking on a man unmoving in overalls.

Ahead was Adam Pritchett staring down, and a man and a woman kneeling with their backs to her. She moved quickly to look over their shoulders.

She struggled for air seeing Stephen lying there.

But his eyes were open and clear. He smiled when seeing her. "Jen, it's okay. Just a graze on the shoulder."

Tears formed in her eyes.

He reassured, "Trust me."

She nodded, unable to get words out. Then she gently replaced the man in holding a bloodstained cloth to her husband's wound.

Pritchett still looked on with his mouth open.

A voice called out from the ground in front of the stage. “We need help here. Please, an EMT. Someone.”

Pritchett looked out at the man yelling, and then walked, seemingly without thinking, across the stage, and down the stairs. He approached the man, a priest, cradling a woman’s head. Blood drenched her white-laced shirt.

Ron McDermott said, “I hear the sirens, Maureen, just hang on a bit. The EMTs will be here very shortly.”

She actually smiled at him. “Father, I don’t think they’ll get here in time.”

Pritchett stared down at her with a quizzical look. “Maureen?”

She struggled to focus. “Adam? Yes, Adam. I forgive you.” She coughed, and blood leaked from the side of her mouth.

The snow, which had been constant for hours, suddenly ceased.

Ron made the sign of the cross on Maureen’s forehead, and declared, “Through this holy unction, may the Lord pardon thee whatever sins or faults thou hast committed. Amen.”

Her eyes went vacant, and Father Ron McDermott gently closed the young woman’s eyelids.

Pritchett whispered, “Forgiven?” He staggered away, and fell into the arms of his security men.

Chapter 42

Pastor Grant and Cardinal Capriano were put in the same hospital room. The NYPD insisted on keeping two guards in the hallway just outside.

This oversized hospital room became a kind of Grand Central Station for assorted metropolitan area Christians. They came with well wishes and blessings for Grant with his deep flesh wound to his shoulder, and for Capriano with the leg and wrist that broke due to his fall from the stage.

Jennifer, along with the Cardinal's brother and sister-in-law, Mickey and Liz, served as quasi-hosts.

The list of visitors from the late morning on was lengthy, and included Dr. Brett Matthews, the FBI's Rich Noack, Paige Caldwell and Charlie Driessen, Sean McEnany with his wife, Rachel, other parishioners at St. Mary's, Pastor Bruce Ericsson, and a long line of Cardinal Capriano's friends, family, staff and fellow Catholic clergy members – from a fellow cardinal to local parish priests.

Pastor Zack Charmichael and Cara Stone arrived and left together, generating smiles from both Stephen and Jennifer.

Father Tom Stone, Maggie Stone and Father Ron McDermott arrived together late in the afternoon. When Ron spoke of Maureen Donahue, the tone shifted. He relayed her last moments.

Maggie said, to no one in particular, "So young."

Jennifer whispered, "I've been thinking about her since last night. She probably saved my life."

Capriano added, "I'm going to speak with her parents tonight, I hope."

A few moments of silence ended with a shock. Mayor-elect Adam Pritchett appeared in the doorway.

He asked, "Do you mind if I come in?"

Stephen actually was speechless, which rarely happened. But Capriano said, "Of course, Mr. Pritchett, please do."

The others in the room found awkward excuses to leave, with Stephen nodding that it was okay for Jennifer to step out. The door was closed behind them.

Pritchett stood uncomfortably between the two hospital beds.

Stephen thought how striking it was for this normally self-assured, arrogant man to be looking down at the floor, unable to muster the strength to look either himself or Capriano in the eye.

The Cardinal said, "Why don't you pull over a chair, and sit down?"

Pritchett did so. Now, he sat just as awkwardly as he had been standing.

Stephen finally found his voice, "How are you, Mr. Pritchett, after yesterday?"

His response was slow. "Well, physically, I'm fine. But I'm wrestling with a lot mentally."

Stephen replied, "Well, being a target of gunmen, and finding oneself in the midst of a large gunfight can have that effect."

Pritchett was still looking down, now at his fidgeting hands. "No, it's not that. I'm trying to figure out why you did what you did, and what Ms. Donahue did."

Stephen asked, "What do you mean?"

Pritchett finally looked directly at Stephen. "You pushed me out of the way when the shooting started. And then ... well ... why in the world did you stand between that gunman and me? You refused to move, and got shot as a result. You literally took a bullet for me. Why would you do that? And when Maureen lay dying on the ground. She looked at me, and said, 'I forgive you.' Why would she say that? I don't understand. I was the reason she was there. I am the reason she's dead. And it was clear that she knew she was dying, and yet, she forgave me. I don't understand. Even you, Cardinal Capriano. I was the enemy, and yet, you let me speak. You trusted me. Why would any of you do any of this?"

Stephen recognized the pain and anguish on the man's face.

Capriano replied, "I think it's safe to say that none of us could do this on our own. From what I've been told about Ms. Donahue, she had been – well, for lack of a better word – renewed in her faith. She found the kindness to forgive through the Holy Spirit. As for myself, after all we've been through on these issues of religious liberty, I know it was the Holy Spirit that gave me the openness to welcome you on stage last night because part of me was working to rebel against any such notion."

Pritchett was looking down at his hands again.

Stephen added, "Mr. Pritchett, I have what some have called a rather unique background. It includes military, intelligence, and pastoral training. I can't tell you how much of each led to my actions last night. But all of that somehow combined, and yes, with the Holy Spirit's help, I just did what I did."

Capriano added, "In each instance, the right thing, hopefully, was done. And that's pretty rare. We humans, including, I know this human" – he used his non-injured hand to point at himself – "too often come up short in what we should do."

Pritchett said, "Well, I thank each of you." He took a deep breath. "And I hope that somehow the two of you can forgive me for all the trouble that I caused."

Stephen replied, "Already forgiven."

Pritchett just shook his head, and in a barely audible voice said, "Thank you, so much. Pastor Grant, how will I ever be able to repay you?"

"You don't have to, in any way, Mr. Pritchett."

Pritchett's eyes moistened. He turned to Capriano. "Cardinal Capriano, I was wondering if you might find some private time with me. I need to talk to someone about many things, about many ... um ... sins."

"Of course, Mr. Pritchett. I believe I'm scheduled to go home tomorrow. Why don't you stop by the residence tomorrow night? We could have dinner and then we can talk."

Pritchett said. " You are so kind. I appreciate that. You have no idea. And I hope that you two might feel comfortable enough to one day call me Adam."

Capriano said, "Adam, it is."

Stephen nodded his assent as well.

Pritchett got up from the chair. "I'm going to go now, so your family and friends can return. Good-bye, and thank you again, Pastor Grant, Cardinal Capriano."

His awkward bewilderment was still evident.

Once he exited the room, Grant and Capriano remained in silence for a few seconds.

Stephen observed, "I think we might just have seen a Christmas miracle, Francis. What do you think?"

Capriano chuckled. "I pray you are right, Stephen."

Chapter 43

In the small farm town north of Minneapolis-St. Paul sat the white-shingled St. Ansgar Catholic Church. Neither the town nor the church had ever seen such an influx of people from New York City before.

Normally, this might have unnerved even the local stoic town and farm families. But their focus was on a huge loss for such a little place. The murder of one of their own, Maureen Donahue, the bright and beautiful daughter of Bernadette and Shelby, and sister to Mark.

Among those exiting the church after the funeral Mass were Stephen and Jennifer, Tom and Maggie Stone, and Ron McDermott. More surprising, perhaps, were the two men coming out next to each other – Cardinal Francis Capriano and Adam Pritchett.

A day earlier, Pritchett had announced his decision to not become mayor of New York City. He said, "My actions and arrogance have caused far too much horror, including the deaths of innocent people. I will spend the rest of my life trying to make up for what cannot be made up for. New York City deserves far more than I could ever give it. I, once again, apologize to the people who were injured, to the families who lost loved ones, to this greatest of all cities, and to others across the nation. I am deeply ashamed."

Behind the dark hearse and limousines was a long line of cars, SUVs and pickups.

As Capriano and Pritchett walked along the line of vehicles, Pritchett said, "These are good people. I cannot believe how they have welcomed me, given what I have done and what I brought down on them."

Capriano replied, "Adam, keep in mind, it wasn't you that shot and killed Maureen. It was that cult leader, Morrison and his followers."

Pritchett said, "I didn't pull the trigger, but I helped load the guns." He switched gears. "Thank you, once more, for everything, Your Eminence. I have to head back to the airport, but we'll see each other on Sunday, correct?"

"Yes, Adam. Safe journey, and God bless you."

With his aide, the Cardinal ducked into their rental car. Pritchett's was parked over a cross street, and several more cars beyond.

But before he reached the silver sedan, a scruffy looking man with a hat and sunglasses emerged from behind a large hill of plowed, Minnesota snow.

The man said, "Adam."

Pritchett stopped, and looked at the individual. Recognition and then concern crossed his face. "Carter, is that you?"

"Yes, it's me," Dujas spat from beneath long blond hair.

"Carter, what happened? Listen, you have to..."

Pritchett's former aide interrupted, "I only have to do one thing." He pulled a handgun out of the pocket of his long, shabby coat, and he pointed it at Pritchett's face. "You are a son-of-a-bitch coward and traitor. It all still could have worked, if you had not quit. You're pathetic, and make me sick."

Pritchett replied, "I know you're angry, Carter. But I can help you. We can get you help."

"Like I said, pathetic." He pulled the trigger, and Adam Pritchett fell back onto the sidewalk.

The gunshot drew the attention of nearly everyone that had come out of St. Ansgar's. Two local police officers, who had been handling traffic matters, drew their service revolvers, each probably for the first time in his career, and rushed in the direction of Dujas. Close behind was Grant.

Dujas just stood watching their approach, tilting his head. As they got closer, he opened his mouth, placed the gun barrel on his tongue, and pulled the trigger.

When the two officers and Grant stopped over the bodies, part of each man's head was absent, and blood rushed out, staining and melting the snow.

Chapter 44

With Jennifer driving, Stephen rode home from the Epiphany evening service at St. Mary's not saying much. He shifted his arm to avoid irritating his still-healing wound, but it was more instinct as his mind was elsewhere.

She asked, "Okay, so what's eating at you?"

"What do you mean?"

"Stephen, come on, I know when you're wrestling with something, big or little. Is this one big or small?"

She knows me well.

He said, "I was going to go in a different direction with the sermon tonight, and I'm not sure if I made the right choice."

"And where were you going to go?"

"My intention was to kind of wrap up the whole religious liberty thing by pointing out that Christians have been confronted by governments seeking to silence them from the very beginning, with King Herod trying to deceive the wise men when it came to the birth of Christ, so that he could silence, you know, kill Jesus as a baby."

Jennifer nodded. "Yes, I can see how that would work. Why didn't you go that route?"

He thought some. "Given that I had spoken about the topic several times over the past few weeks, I decided that maybe it should be time to take a break from the pulpit.

I'm just not sure if I dropped the ball, if I missed an opportunity."

It was Jennifer's turn to reflect. "Well, why don't you just take the sermon you didn't give, write it up for the church website and for the next newsletter? In addition, why not take some of that material the Synod has about religious liberty online, including those excellent television commercials, and do a class?"

Stephen glanced at his wife, smiled, and shook his head.

She asked, "What? Why the head shake?"

"Because I'm sitting here going through internal angst over something that had a straightforward answer that you just provided. It's not the first time you've done that for me, and it won't be the last."

Jennifer replied, "Darn right, it won't be the last."

Jennifer parked the red Chevy Tahoe on the circular driveway outside their home.

After they got out, Jennifer said, "I've done something else for you."

"And what is that?" He was intrigued.

"We really didn't have any Christmas alone time."

"We did not, Mrs. Grant."

"And I know that yesterday was the twelfth day of Christmas, but my family always referred to Epiphany as Little Christmas growing up."

"As did mine."

"I finished up work early today, and got things ready for our own Little Christmas tonight. Can you wait out here for five minutes?"

Stephen could see how excited she was. "For this, of course. Actually, I'm going to go rummage around in the garage, and you can let me know when the light is green."

Five minutes later, Jennifer opened the front door slightly, and called to Stephen, "Okay, come in."

He shut the garage, crossed the driveway, and entered the house. He immediately smiled, and asked, "How?"

"Well, you missed *White Christmas* this year, so I wanted to make this special."

She was standing in the middle of their living room dressed in a replica of the red gown with white fur trim worn by Vera-Ellen at the end of the film as she, Rosemary Clooney, Danny Kaye and Bing Crosby sang "White Christmas."

For good measure, their Christmas tree had been taken down and replaced with one bathed in tinsel, just like in the movie as well.

On the television screen, the menu for *White Christmas* waited for someone to click "Play."

He walked over, and said. "You look beautiful."

Jennifer stepped back, and ran her hands down the dress. "Do really you think so?" She smiled. "I have to say that I really do love it. A client from California got me in contact with the right people. It's fun."

They kissed.

Stephen observed, "I always wondered what it would be like to kiss Vera-Ellen."

Jennifer said, "I bet you have. And who knows what might happen after the movie."

"This is turning out to be the best Little Christmas ever."

"Before you get too carried away, sit down, my dear." She pushed him down on the couch, sat down as well, loosened his collar, poured two glasses of wine, grabbed the remote, and clicked play. But before she could get comfortable, Stephen reached out and touched her cheek.

He said, "Thank you." And he kissed her gently on the lips.

"And thank you, Stephen, for being my protector and my love."

She moved next to him as the movie started.

Stephen couldn't resist. "As Danny Kaye says to Vera-Ellen after they kissed in this very movie, 'You know, in some ways, you're far superior to my cocker spaniel.'"

She drove an elbow into his ribs.

"Okay, I deserved that."

"Yes, you did," Jennifer said, as she moved in even closer to her husband. "And by the way, I've never wondered what it would be like to kiss Danny Kaye, so you might want to drop that line, if you want to get lucky later."

"Danny who? It's already dropped."

About the Author

This is Ray Keating's third novel featuring Stephen Grant. The first was *Warrior Monk: A Pastor Stephen Grant Novel*, followed by *Root of All Evil? A Pastor Stephen Grant Novel*.

Keating also is a weekly columnist with the Dolan Company (including *Long Island Business News* and other newspapers), a former *Newsday* weekly columnist, an economist, an adjunct college professor, and board member of the American Lutheran Publicity Bureau. His work has appeared in a wide range of additional periodicals, including *The New York Times, The Wall Street Journal, The Washington Post, New York Post,* Los Angeles *Daily News, The Boston Globe, National Review, The Washington Times*, *Investor's Business Daily*, New York *Daily News, Detroit Free Press, Chicago Tribune, Providence Journal Bulletin,* and *Cincinnati Enquirer*. Keating lives on Long Island with his family.

Made in the USA
Charleston, SC
08 July 2014